"Let me stay with you."

Lyssa spun around. "Stay with me? Why?"

Alex closed the distance between them. He cupped her chin and forced her to look at him. "I want to stay with you to protect you. As your husband."

For a moment she appeared to soften. Then she pulled away. "You never were really my husband—you know that. Your duty to me—if you ever even had one—is officially over."

He stared, making his expression equally hard and determined. "There's a serial killer in the area. Surely you can't think—?"

"He tried for me." She lifted her chin, the slight tremor in her voice belying her attempt to appear nonchalant. "He failed. I'm okay. You came all the way out here for nothing." She pushed a few wayward strands of hair from her face. "Go away, Alex. I'm not your responsibility."

"I'm not going anywhere," he growled.

Dear Reader,

Get ready for this month's romantic adrenaline rush from Silhouette Intimate Moments. First up, we have RITA® Award-winning author Kathleen Creighton's next STARRS OF THE WEST book, *Secret Agent Sam* (#1363), a high-speed, action-packed romance with a tough-as-nails heroine you'll never forget. RaeAnne Thayne delivers the next book in her emotional miniseries THE SEARCHERS, *Never Too Late* (#1364), which details a heroine's search for the truth about her mysterious past...and an unexpected detour in love.

As part of Karen Whiddon's intriguing series THE PACK— about humans who shape-shift into wolves—*One Eye Closed* (#1365) tells the story of a wife who is in danger and turns to the only man who can help: her enigmatic husband. Kylie Brant heats up our imagination in *The Business of Strangers* (#1366), where a beautiful amnesiac falls for the last man on earth she should love— a reputed enemy!

Linda Randall Wisdom enthralls us with *After the Midnight Hour* (#1367), a story of a heart-stopping detective's fierce attraction to a tormented woman...who was murdered by her husband a century ago! Can this impossible love overcome the bonds of time? And don't miss Loreth Anne White's *The Sheik Who Loved Me* (#1368), in which a dazzling spy falls for the sexy sheik she's supposed to be investigating. So, what will win out—duty or true love?

Live and love the excitement in Silhouette Intimate Moments, where emotion meets high-stakes romance. And be sure to join us next month for another stellar lineup.

Happy reading!

Patience Smith
Associate Senior Editor

Please address questions and book requests to:
Silhouette Reader Service
U.S.: 3010 Walden Ave., P.O. Box 1325, Buffalo, NY 14269
Canadian: P.O. Box 609, Fort Erie, Ont. L2A 5X3

One Eye Closed
KAREN WHIDDON

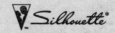

INTIMATE MOMENTS™
Published by Silhouette Books
America's Publisher of Contemporary Romance

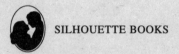 **SILHOUETTE BOOKS**

ISBN 0-373-27435-1

ONE EYE CLOSED

Visit Silhouette Books at www.eHarlequin.com

Printed in U.S.A.

Books by Karen Whiddon

Intimate Moments

One Eye Open #1301
One Eye Closed #1365

*The Pack

KAREN WHIDDON

started weaving fanciful tales for her younger brothers at the age of eleven. Amidst first the Catskill Mountains of New York and then the Rocky Mountains of Colorado, she fueled her imagination with the natural beauty of the rugged peaks and spun stories of love that captivated her family's attention.

Karen now lives in North Texas, where she shares her life with her very own hero of a husband and three doting dogs. Also an entrepreneur, she divides her time between the business she started and writing the contemporary romantic suspense and paranormal romances that readers enjoy and that she now brings to Silhouette Intimate Moments. You can e-mail Karen at KWhiddon1@aol.com or write to her at P.O. Box 820807, Fort Worth, TX 76182. Fans of her writing can also check out her Web site at www.KarenWhiddon.com.

Dedicated as always to the love of my life, Lonnie.

And since you never asked, this one is also
for Tom and Nancy Cooper—and let's not forget Amie.

Finally, a special thanks to my friend
and the Best Critique Partner ever, Anna Adams.

Prologue

"Home run!" The sportscaster's excited voice sounded far away, even though the volume on the big-screen TV was turned to ear-breaking levels.

Alex Lupe stood, stumbling. He ran his shaky hand across his forehead, suddenly beaded with sweat.

"You all right, buddy?" His best friend, Carson Turner, squinted up at him.

"I don't—"

"Take it easy. The inning's nearly over. Your Red Sox just scored."

Trying to focus on the game, Alex shook his head. "No." He felt a sharp jab of terror, a bright sunburst of pain. Strong hands squeezed his throat, no air—he couldn't breathe. Not here, not in Carson's comfortable den with a half-eaten pepperoni pizza still warm on the coffee table. But somewhere, right now—

Panic. Fear. Shock. Alex bared his teeth. Growled.

Lyssa. His wife. In danger.

Alex staggered, his breath coming in short, heaving gasps. Then, as suddenly as it had begun, air flooded his lungs, his vision cleared. *Safe.* The awful feeling passed.

"I'm all right," he managed to say, lying to his friend.

"Hey." Carson held up his phone. "I was about to call 9-1-1. What happened? You look like you've seen a ghost."

Alex used all his willpower to keep from clawing at his throat. "I have," he said, hearing a faint echo of horror remaining in his own voice. "Lyssa's in trouble. Someone just tried to kill her."

"How do you know?"

Alex swallowed. "I felt her. Just now."

To his credit, Carson didn't react with disbelief. Since marrying Alex's sister, he'd learned there were many unknown aspects to life. He simply nodded, his law-enforcement training kicking in. "What are you going to do?"

"I'm going up there. Now."

Chapter 1

A crash from the reception area made everyone turn. The Wicket Hollow police station was usually closed this time of night. Everyone in town knew that. The overeager reporters who'd been camped out front had finally gone back to the Red Inn Motel. They'd gotten all of the story they were likely to until tomorrow.

Lyssa Reinholt-Lupe shivered. Not from cold, but because the back of her neck tingled a familiar warning.

"I'm sure that door is locked." Officer Kane frowned.

They all heard a sharp crack, then the unmistakable sound of glass shattering.

"What the—" The two local cops rushed forward, guns drawn. Officer Kane darted a quick look at Lyssa and followed. Four of the FBI agents moved near Lyssa, enclosing her in a protective circle. While they did not draw their weapons, their holsters were readily accessible. The other two, including Special Agent Trask, waited in the back of the room, looking bored.

"Lyssa." A male voice bellowed. Lyssa gasped. She recognized that voice. Always would. Despite her best efforts, the sound of it still haunted her dreams.

Now her impromptu guards armed themselves, weapons aimed at the door.

"Wait. That's…Alex?" Heart pounding, Lyssa started forward, only to be blocked by a frowning FBI agent.

"Do you know that guy?"

Know him? She'd married him two years, eleven months and ten days ago, not that she was counting or anything. Though their impromptu marriage had started out only as a means to protect her from her sister's gang's initiation rites, technically they were still husband and wife. Neither had bothered to take the necessary steps to dissolve it.

"He's my husband." She shoved at the agent with one hand. "Let me through. I can take care of myself."

The man looked skeptical. "Maybe you can. Maybe you can't. Do you know him?"

Still intent on pushing past him, she opened her mouth to speak. But the night's events—assault, near-death, rescue, interrogation, and now this—finally took their toll.

The edges of her vision blurred, then grayed. She staggered, then stumbled, before everything went black.

Why'd they put me in jail? Alex glared at the black iron bars and waited for the constable or sheriff or whoever was in charge in this Podunk little town to arrive so he could get his single phone call. They'd taken his cell phone and wallet when they'd locked him in this place.

Worst of all, they hadn't been impressed when he told them who he was. They'd taken his ID, proof positive he was a federal agent—DEA to be specific—but still they'd refused to let him see Lyssa. He'd been cooling his heels here for well over an hour, fuming. When these locals finally got around to letting him out, heads were gonna roll.

Instead, four government agents paid him a visit. He recognized one of them, a tall, dour man with close-cropped graying hair.

"Never thought I'd see you here, Lupe." The FBI agent Alex knew as Trask unlocked his cell door. He indicated the other men. "FBI. All of us."

"Why am I here?"

The other man raised a graying brow. "Why the hell did you try to pick a fight with two armed locals? There are more conventional methods of gaining entry than trying to force your way in without answering questions. You broke the door, too."

"They wouldn't let me in." Knowing he sounded surly, Alex produced a smile. "Even when I told them who I was."

"Really?" Trask handed Alex back his ID. "DEA hasn't been called in on this case and, even if they had been, you're on leave."

"I'm not here on DEA business. I'm here to see Lyssa." Alex fought the urge to bare his teeth. "My wife."

"Your what?" The other man's lined face creased even more in puzzlement. "When did you get married?"

"A few years ago, when I was undercover in Hades Claws. Lyssa joined the gang trying to get her sister out. I could tell she didn't belong there. Any unmarried woman was fresh meat to them—they believed in sharing." He knew his tight-lipped smile looked savage, but didn't care. "Lyssa's sister didn't mind. Lyssa did."

"So you felt sorry for her and married her." Trask shook his head. "You always had a reputation for helping the underdog, but this—" He laughed. "So are you still married? Or did you divorce her once the case was finished?"

Conscious of the other men's avid interest, Alex clenched his teeth. "None of your business."

"You're not together anymore."

"She left the gang when she realized her sister wouldn't. I had to stay and wrap things up." He glared at Trask. "I need to see my wife."

"She doesn't want to see you." Agent Number Two stepped forward. "She passed out when she heard your voice."

"Passed *out?* Is she okay?"

"Exhaustion. She'll be fine as long as you stay away."

"Did *she* say that?"

"No."

"Of course not."

Alex continued to stare at Trask.

Trask looked back, expressionless.

Stalemate.

Checking his watch, Alex let the other man win. This time. He grimaced. "I'll pay for the door. I need to go. Now."

"Wait a minute." Trask crossed his arms. "Alex, you were undercover for a long time."

"Yeah, so?"

"Sometimes men who've been under that long lose track of what's acceptable behavior."

"Look—" Alex exploded "—I—"

"Taking a swing at uniformed locals isn't—"

"I know." Dragging his hand across his mouth, Alex exhaled. "I made an error in judgment. I'm worried about my wife."

"I'm trying to help you. Sure, we've ruled you out as a suspect—"

"*Suspect?*"

Trask continued as if Alex hadn't interrupted. "But your behavior here indicates to me that you need to talk to someone. Surely the DEA can refer you."

"I already said I'd pay for the damn door."

"What about your wife? Are you gonna stay away from her?"

Grim-jawed, Alex said nothing.

This time, Trask looked away first. "Look, I've seen her. She's damn gorgeous, so I can't say I blame you. But she's been through a rough time." He shook his head. "She was nearly killed. This UNSUB is bad news. If she hadn't escaped, Lyssa would have been his fifth victim. You need to think about that."

"That's why I'm here. To protect her."

Consulting his clipboard, Trask finally smiled. Like Alex's, his expression contained no trace of humor. "That's why *we're* here. She's under protective custody. We want to move her to a safe house as soon as we can. Right now she refuses to leave her home."

Alex stared. "Protective custody I can understand, but a safe house? Why?"

"The profiler thinks this guy will try again."

That did it. He had to get to Lyssa. "Trask, while it's good to see you again, I've got to go. I'll check with you later."

The other man moved to block the door.

"You move quickly for such an old guy." Alex flashed his best "I'm harmless" grin.

Trask didn't fall for it. "We've got a file on this guy. Do you want to see it?"

"Yeah. But not now. Later. Right now I've got to get to Lyssa."

The other man didn't move from the doorway. "It's been a while since you've seen her, hasn't it?"

"Not that long. I came to her sister's funeral."

"Right." Trask consulted his notes. "Claire Reinholt. Another Hades Claws member. Murdered. That was what, three months ago?"

"Yes." Alex forced himself to unclench his teeth. "Lyssa wanted to see me then. She'll be glad to see me now, despite what she says." He gave the FBI agent another hard look. "If you'd kindly get out of my way so I can go."

"It's late. She's had a tough night, she needs to sleep."

"Fine. You have my word I'll wait until morning."

"You're not being charged with anything." Trask stepped aside. "You can go. But try to stay out of trouble, okay?"

Moving forward, Alex remembered enough of the niceties to shake the other man's hand. "I will. Thanks."

"Yeah. Leave your information at the front desk. They'll want to send you a bill for the door frame."

The next morning, as he drove down Main Street, Alex checked his own notes on the serial killer. He'd downloaded them while waiting at the airport. Dubbed the Catskill Killer by the press, the FBI had taken to calling him the Bone Man due to his habit of removing a rib from each of his victims. The UNSUB—unknown subject—was vicious, undisciplined and growing more and more ritualistic.

Aspects of his MO bothered Alex. If he didn't know better, he'd think the Bone Man was a shape-shifter gone berserk. Especially with the rib thing—he remembered an old legend in which some ancient shape-shifter king had created an immortal queen from a human woman's rib. Could some modern-day crazy be trying to imitate the old story? Either way, shape-shifter or human, the killer was dangerous.

Worse, this guy had nearly gotten Lyssa.

Though their marriage hadn't been real, Alex felt responsible. Even though their marriage started out as a necessity, he'd come to care for Lyssa. While they'd lived together under the watchful eyes of the gang, she'd continued to try and get her sister to leave while Alex had continued his undercover role. Undercover—even to her. He'd had nearly enough information to bring the gang down, but was trying to learn who'd killed his partner, Carson's, family.

Then, eighteen months ago and more than a year after they married, Lyssa had told him she was leaving. Alex hid his dismay, knowing that letting her go was the right thing to do, even as he'd wanted to beg her to stay. Instead, he'd watched her leave without a word, shouldering another burden when he'd promised he'd try to look after Claire.

Shortly before the Hades Claws sting had drawn to a close, Claire was found dead, brutally murdered. Though he hadn't seen Lyssa in more than a year, Alex had attended Claire's funeral. Seeing Lyssa again, comforting her, had sent both their emotions spiraling out of control. Bad for him, even worse for her, as he'd had to leave her again without a word of explanation.

Even when the investigation ended, Alex had stayed away. Not from desire, but from fear. He had an even bigger secret than his status as an undercover agent. A secret he was afraid to share with anyone, especially the woman who remained his wife. Oh, he knew he had no true claim to her. Not anymore. Still, just the thought of the killer's hands around her neck infuriated him.

And now Trask indicated this guy would try again.

Alex had to find Lyssa. His insides churned. He'd barely wrapped up the Hades Claws case, taking advantage of some well-earned downtime, when he'd felt her being attacked. Felt, as if he'd been inside her skin.

That scared the hell out of him and, at the same time, intrigued him. Such connections existed only rarely among his kind, and then only between true mates. No matter that she was human and he was not, or that their marriage was not real—before God and witnesses, he'd named her *wife*. Now, he would protect her.

Maybe by doing so he could appease the guilt he felt at hurting her so badly.

Keeping his '63 Corvette to a slow purr, he drove through Wicket Hollow, New York. Though the downtown storefronts had been restored, the place had the feel of a ghost town. Old-fashioned. As though the people were leaning toward the past rather than the future. It reminded him of Leaning Tree, his own hometown.

Then he saw the rustic, green building with its hand-painted sign. *Gardening Haven.* Lyssa's shop. She'd mentioned it more than once during the brief time they'd actually lived in the same place.

Parking his car in front, he went inside.

Letting his eyes adjust to the dim interior, he tried to detect her scent. He smelled damp earth and growing things, the faintly acrid odor of bagged manure and other fertilizers, but not the sweet floral scent of his wife.

A petite, dark-haired woman stood behind the counter.

"Can I help you?" Openly, she checked him out, her smile widening as though she liked what she saw.

"I'm looking for Lyssa."

Her smile dimmed. "They all are, honey. Why won't you people leave her alone?"

You people? Alex simply stared.

Something in his face must have communicated his confusion to her. She squinted up at him. "Aren't you a reporter?"

"No." Damn, he'd forgotten about them. Lyssa's attack had made national news. "I'm her husband."

"Her husband?" Rearing back, she repeated the words, this time loudly enough to draw the attention of another woman, who hustled around the corner and came to a halt at the counter. Wide-eyed, they gaped at him like he'd suddenly sprouted two heads, making him wonder exactly what Lyssa had told them about him.

"Her husband," the brunette repeated, a hushed quality to her voice. "After all this time."

"Yeah. I came up from the city." Pasting a skeptical expression on his face, he cocked his head. "Didn't I meet you both at Claire's funeral?"

The new arrival, a slender blonde with close-cropped hair, waggled a finger at him. "You did, but that was nearly three months ago. You disappeared again right after that. I'm thinking you should call yourself *ex-husband* instead."

"We haven't filed for divorce." He glared at her.

"Only because she can't afford it."

"Marilee!" The first woman sounded shocked, yet continued to glare in a decidedly unfriendly way. He supposed he ought to be glad Lyssa had such staunch friends to support her, but he was bone tired. He needed to see his wife.

"Marilee." He drew out her name. "You took care of the shop while Lyssa was in Welkory with me."

She nodded, a quick dip of her head. "Yes. I was surprised it took her so long to come to her senses."

"This is really none of your business."

Marilee flushed. "Sorry. I guess maybe you're right. I'm not usually so rude, but Lyssa is my best friend. I care about her. You hurt her. I don't want her hurt again, particularly after what she's been through."

"I don't want her hurt either." And he meant it, though if his staying and protecting her now would bring her pain, she'd have to learn to deal with it. No way was he leaving her unprotected.

Marilee eyed him the way a she-wolf eyes a strange female wanting to nose around her cubs. "What are you doing here? What do you want?"

Direct. Alex liked direct. It saved time. He looked from one woman to the other. "I need to see my wife."

Neither woman moved. Marilee actually crossed her arms and glared at him as though daring him to go through her.

So much for direct. He cursed under his breath. "Ladies, I don't have time for this—" He reached in his pocket and flashed his badge, knowing at this distance they couldn't read which division of law enforcement it showed. "I'm here to protect my wife."

"You're with the FBI?" Marilee's voice rang with shock, telling him his Hades Claws persona still existed in her mind.

"The FBI," the other woman repeated, eyeing him with suspicion. "I don't believe it."

Pocketing his badge, he didn't correct her. DEA, FBI, to a civilian they were much the same.

The brunette shook her head. "Lyssa's already talked to the FBI and the police. She has their protection."

"Not enough. She needs me."

"Or you need her." Marilee gave him a wry grin, apparently having made up her mind about something. "Pretty desperate, aren't you?" She actually winked, and he realized she'd convinced herself he was here for some other, more romantic, reason.

Fine. Let her think he was lovesick. He didn't give a damn. If that's what it took…he'd play along.

"Desperate doesn't begin to describe it," he growled. All he wanted to do was get Lyssa away to someplace safe. "Now will you tell me where my wife is?"

Both women stared at him. Finally Marilee laughed and waved her hand toward the back. "You wait here. Let me go get her. She's out back in the garden. I want to make sure she wants to see—"

"That's okay. Thanks." Shouldering his way past her toward the open doorway, he stepped outside, ignoring her sputtering protests. Shading his eyes against the bright sunlight, he spotted her.

Lyssa's golden hair glowed bright in the morning sun. She had her back to him, bent over the plants talking, a peculiar habit of hers that had earned her a lot of grief from the other members of Hades Claws. She'd simply smiled, saying simple conversation helped all green things grow. From the thriving nursery area around her, he almost believed her.

Moving toward the woman who was still legally his wife, he felt predatory, more like himself than he'd felt in months.

Hearing footsteps, she straightened and lifted her head. Her gaze flew to his and she froze, like a young doe that's ventured too close to a highway.

"Alex." One word, no inflection. Quite a bit different from the way she'd greeted him three months ago.

Pushing away the thought, he studied her face, noting her hollowed cheeks and pain-filled green eyes.

While she didn't flinch at his perusal, the intensity of his stare made her turn her head.

"Lyssa. You look tired." Bad thing to say. As soon as the words left his mouth, he wanted to recall them. He winced at the hurt that flashed across her face.

Lyssa shook her head, sending her thick blond braid flying. "Tired? I guess I am. I was nearly killed last night." She crossed her arms, as though she felt the need to shield her body from his gaze. "But then you know that. Why are you here now? Because I was attacked?"

He made his expression professional. "Can we go somewhere and talk?"

She looked down, then up, fixing her gaze on a point somewhere above and to the left of his head. He found it interesting that she wouldn't look at him directly.

"Not now." Clenching her hands together, she tried to hide her trembling. Like always, Lyssa wanted to appear tough. "I need to be alone for a little while. Once I finish here, I'm going home to take a nap."

He could see how badly she needed to rest by the shadows under her eyes. Still, selfishly, he didn't want to leave. Not as long as she wasn't safe. He didn't analyze his need to protect her; protecting people was what he did, why he'd chosen law enforcement as a career in the first place. She was still his wife. He'd protect her. End of story. "I'll drive you home."

"No. I live here." She jerked her head in the direction of a quaint, wood-frame bungalow, painted the same pale shade of green as the store. "I can walk."

Confusion, anger, grief, all of these he heard in her voice. She still mourned her sister, he knew. Now that his investigation was over, maybe he could help appease some of that particular heartache.

"Nemo was arrested. Drugs, money laundering, several other charges. He's behind bars, awaiting trial." Nemo had been her sister Claire's boyfriend, the one who'd gotten her hooked on crack cocaine and the reason she'd joined the gang in the first place.

Lyssa jerked her head once, a quick nod. "I know. I saw it on the news."

He heard no happiness or relief in her voice. And, since she'd already turned away, he couldn't see her expression.

Taking a step toward her, he thought better of it. "I thought you'd be glad."

"I didn't see murder listed among the charges." She sounded fierce. Staring at her hunched shoulders, he felt the backlash of her sorrow. Claire had been murdered. Nemo had been the prime suspect.

"There wasn't enough evidence to get a conviction. No one knows for sure he killed your sister."

"Who else?" Spinning around to glare at him, she grimaced. "It had to be him."

"There wasn't enough for an indictment. I'm sorry. I know you miss her."

"Yes." She looked away, pain shadowing her pale face. He gave her a moment, watching as she straightened her shoulders and collected herself. Becoming what she thought others needed. Strong again.

Finally she lifted her chin, meeting his gaze, her expression cool, though she wasn't entirely successful in hiding her grief. "I do miss Claire. I'm glad that SOB is in jail, but nothing can bring her back."

For the first time, he wondered if she blamed him for her sister's gruesome death. Alex hadn't been able to save her. No one could have been able to foretell Claire's violent end. Though Nemo swore innocence, Alex wished he could have made sure he'd stand trial on murder charges. But even the D.A. had been doubtful. There was nothing but gut feeling to tie Nemo to Claire's death.

Discussing the unsolved crime only brought back bad memories. As did his presence. Without even trying, he'd managed to hurt her again when all he'd wanted to do was help.

As though she shared his thoughts, Lyssa frowned. "I've got to go. I can't deal with you now." Turning her back to him, she started up the path.

His stomach clenched, just like it always did when a drug bust was about to go sour. He supposed he deserved it. "Lyssa, wait."

Ignoring him, she kept walking.

"Let me stay with you."

She spun around, her expression shocked. "Stay with me? Why?"

He knew she was remembering the last time he'd

stayed with her. She'd thought he'd come back to her for good, to make their marriage real. He hadn't corrected her, though he knew he had to go back to Welkory, back to the Claws so he could wrap up the undercover operation. *Lies.* Yes, he definitely deserved her wariness. But he had no choice. Telling falsehoods and playing a role were all part of what he did.

With a few steps, he closed the distance between them. Lowering his voice, he cupped her chin and forced her to look at him, really look at him. "I want to stay with you to protect you. As your husband."

For a moment she appeared to soften visibly. Then her mouth tightened. She pulled away. "You never were really my husband—you know that. If I was foolish, stupid even, when you came for Claire's funeral, I'm over that now. You don't have to pretend any longer. Your duty to me—if you ever even had one—is officially over."

"You never divorced me."

She stared, momentarily speechless. "I couldn't afford an attorney."

"I didn't file either. We're still married, Lyssa. Let me help you."

"I took your help once, almost three years ago, because I had no other choice. Since then, I've lost my sister and," she lifted her chin, "my husband. Have me served with papers. I'll sign them."

If he hadn't known her better, he might have believed her no-nonsense voice, the tough look on her face. But he knew Lyssa. Being tough was her way of protecting herself.

He stared, making his expression equally hard and determined. "No divorce. Not now. There's a serial killer after you."

"I know. I was there. He tried for me." The slight tremor in her husky voice contradicted her attempt to appear nonchalant. "He failed. You already know that. I'm okay. You came all the way out here for nothing."

"They think he'll try again."

"I know," she said. "That's why the police insist on staying." She pushed a few wayward strands of her long hair from her face. "Go away, Alex. I'm not your responsibility."

How could he make her understand? In the last two years, he'd failed to protect so many, starting with Carson's family and ending with Claire.

"I'm not going anywhere," he growled, letting her see his frustration, which he instantly realized was a mistake. Intimidation had never worked with her. She simply refused to back down.

"That's your problem then. But you're not staying with me. I've got protection. I've got two uniformed police officers guarding me now."

"Local cops? Where's the FBI?"

"They're around here somewhere." Ignoring him, she began walking. He kept pace, trying to decide if he should try to win her with charm and wondering why he felt too damn tired to make the effort. He wanted to be himself for once, damn it—or as much as he could be when surrounded by humans.

When they reached the back of her house, she turned the knob, slipping inside and keeping the thick wooden door between then. "Goodbye, Alex."

He tried another tack. "We still need to talk. Get some—" he searched for a word she'd empathize with, finding one he'd never under normal circumstances utter "—*closure.*"

This time, to his relief, she nodded. "You're right, we do. And we will, after I sleep." Then she firmly shut the door in his face.

For a moment he simply stood, staring at the peeling paint. *Closure my ass.* He wanted to start over. He wanted a new beginning, not an end.

A uniformed officer materialized at his side. "Can I escort you anywhere, sir?"

The local was young, twenty-two at the most. Alex contemplated flashing his badge and bluffing his way inside Lyssa's house, but knew she'd be royally pissed. Since he needed her cooperation to stay, he figured he'd better play by the rules for now.

Except the rules took up too much time. Lyssa's life was in danger. The hell with the rules. This serial killer, the UNSUB who'd nearly gotten her, wouldn't play by any rules.

"Sir?"

Alex looked from the uniform to the door. One swift run with his shoulder, and he'd bet he could break the flimsy hinges. But he'd already made that mistake once today. He wouldn't make it again.

The door opened again, saving him from having to make a choice.

"Alex?" Her green gaze was direct, her expression fierce and determined.

He flashed the cop an *I told you so* smile. "Yes?"

With a faint lift of her lips, she raised her brows at the officer, who stood his ground. She cleared her throat. Finally, he got the message and stepped back.

Once he'd moved a safe distance, she returned her expression to Alex.

"Why'd you come here? Actions speak louder than

words, Alex. When you left the last time, you made it plain you wanted no part of me or my life. So why come back now? I didn't call you. I don't need you. So why?"

"Because I couldn't stay away." The words exploded from him. "Lyssa, I wanted to tell you before, but—"

She smiled sadly, waiting for him to finish.

He glanced again at the cop, who made no attempt to hide his eavesdropping. "We need to talk." Alex lowered his voice. "There's stuff I couldn't tell you then that I can now."

"Stuff?"

He cursed his lack of eloquence. "Yeah."

"Like the fact that you were undercover DEA?"

He couldn't keep his shock from showing. "You knew?"

"I do now. Trask told me. You know, the bust of Hades Claws was all over the papers, in the news. They didn't name you, or show your face. I figured you went to prison." No inflection or hint of emotion showed in her face, her voice. "I didn't find out the truth until now."

"I couldn't tell you. The investigation wasn't over. It would have been too dangerous for you to know."

"What does it matter?" She didn't move. "I understand that you couldn't risk your cover. I appreciate the way you helped me. But your undercover investigation is over. I was a part of that, of that life. It's done now. Alex, I'm grateful for all you've done, for keeping the gang away from me and trying to help me get Claire out. I'd like to think we became sort of friends through all this. Don't ruin that now."

"Friends?" Hearing her say the word bothered him,

somehow. "We were together as man and wife for more than a year. We were—are—more than friends. We—"

Glancing at the waiting cop, she held up a hand, face coloring. "Don't say it."

"But—"

One delicate brow arched. "Okay, maybe I'm wrong. Maybe we're not friends, just acquaintances."

"No." Frustrated at being reduced to one-word answers, he glared at the hovering policeman, who took another step back. "You're not wrong. We *are* friends." He choked on the word, aware that he had to be careful. To prove to Nemo and the other Claws they were really married, they'd shared a room. Eventually, they'd shared more. Their marriage had been as real as it could be under the circumstances. But she'd never known the real him, the true Alex Lupe. She was right about that—he'd been living a lie. They'd been two broken people who'd found temporary solace in each other's arms.

Which suited him fine. He'd only come here now to keep her safe from a madman. After the Bone Man had been captured, he'd be on his way once more. Back to his real life.

"Yes, we're friends," he repeated.

"Good." Her green eyes gleamed. "So you can go then, *pal*. I'll be fine. You've done enough. I appreciate everything. Really." She twirled a strand of her long, blond hair in her fingers, the nervous gesture at odds with her calm, decisive tone. "Seriously. You can go."

His mouth went dry. He took a deep breath. Set his unwavering gaze. How easily he slipped into the undercover persona, the Alex who dealt calmly with almost any situation.

Except now he could hear his heartbeat thrumming loudly in his ears.

He glared again at the cop, mister ever-watchful. "Can we get a little privacy here?"

The other guy nodded, backing away.

Lyssa crossed her arms. "Well?"

"I had to come. I knew about the attack the instant it happened. Maybe because we got married—wait." He held up his hand. "I know our vows weren't meant to be real. But we consummated our marriage, Lyssa. There's some sort of connection between us. I don't know why, or how. All I know is that I *felt* you. I felt his hands around your throat, trying to squeeze the air from your lungs."

Lyssa jerked back, glaring at him. "Don't play games, Alex. I hate lies. I don't believe in the supernatural."

He went still, something inside him withering. Though she didn't realize it, her words negated him, all he was. His very existence was proof of the paranormal.

Chapter 2

Lyssa clenched her teeth. She didn't trust her responses since the attack. How could she keep up her strong front when Alex's presence amplified the fear and impotent anger that still coursed through her?

Narrowing his eyes, he studied her. "Why don't you believe in things you can't see?"

"I only believe in what I can touch, see, and feel. Call me unimaginative, but I'm only practical. Ever since Claire and I were kids, we had a pact. Whichever of us died first would contact the other, someway, somehow. It was the only one of Claire's fantasies I believed in."

She kept her expression impassive, managing to lift one shoulder in a shrug, as though none of this mattered. "Claire's dead, Alex."

"And you never heard from her."

"No. Nothing. After she died, it was as if she'd never

existed." To her horror her voice thickened. She cleared her throat. "She's gone. Really gone. All of her."

Sympathy shone from his dark gaze. She could take anything but that.

He took a step toward her.

She moved back.

The waiting cop started forward. Lyssa stopped him with a look.

"I'm sorry." Alex had schooled his expression back to his impersonal, "I'm a fed" face. "Lyssa, I'm sorry. I failed you in that. I tried to protect her."

"*You* failed?" Perversely, she wanted to slap his face. "Protecting Claire wasn't your duty, it was mine. She was my baby sister. I went into the Claws to get her out. She refused. I gave up. If anyone failed, I did."

They stared at each other, the silence ringing. His unsmiling regard made her want to weep. Then, as she studied him, the real reason he'd come back to her struck her with the force of an invisible backhanded slap. "Tell me that's not why you're here."

He didn't respond.

"You came back to try and protect me because you think you failed to save Claire." Not a question. She *knew.* "It's not your problem." She crossed her arms. "There. I've absolved you. You can leave now."

He didn't move. His wide-legged stance seemed aggressive to her, though apparently not aggressive enough to alarm the uniformed officer who was supposed to keep her safe.

"I came because I felt you." He shook his head, his expression still stony.

Her jaw hurt from clenching it. "Please stop."

He moved closer, still watching her with that damned

intent focus that had always reminded her of a hunter. Though she hated to, she backed away. If he touched her, she knew she'd shatter.

As if he knew, he cocked his head. "I had a couple of other reasons for coming here. We need to settle this marriage thing, once and for all."

As he'd no doubt known they would, his choice of words intrigued her. They'd been married eighteen months before she'd left the Claws and returned to Wicket Hollow, stupidly thinking he'd eventually follow. Not only had he been unable to leave, he'd not contacted her once after she'd left.

Until Claire had died. Alex's appearance at her sister's funeral had stunned Lyssa. They'd made love, which had given her false hope that this time, he'd stay. She wouldn't make that mistake again.

"I don't care." But this time, she lied, and they both knew it.

"We have to talk." He cocked his head, waiting.

Unsmiling, she opened the door and stepped aside for him to pass. She made sure to give him a wide berth, careful no part of their bodies touched.

He moved past her into her small living room and stopped, as if struck by the vibrant colors. Since her guests often reacted this way, Lyssa wasn't surprised. The room was bright and sunny, just the way she liked it. She'd painted the walls a brilliant yellow, which should have clashed with the blue denim couch and tangerine chair, but didn't. Everywhere one looked was a splash of color, from the vivid, modern paintings to the striped throw rug on the polished wood floor.

"Compared to this, our apartment must have seemed

boring as hell." Finishing his perusal, Alex looked at her, unsmiling.

She didn't answer. He'd become part of her life out of necessity—and she would always be grateful to him for saving her from Nemo and the other Claws. But that was all she felt. Correction—all she'd allow herself to feel. Gratitude, nothing more. The passionate nights they'd spent together would no longer haunt her dreams. They'd never been based on reality, anyway.

Glancing at Alex, she felt heat rise in her face. At least he, despite his claims to the contrary, didn't know what she was thinking. Instead, he seemed preoccupied with her living room.

"I smell…." Lifting his head, Alex sniffed. He made a sound low in his throat, almost a growl. As he did, a fluffy ball of fur launched itself up from the couch, streaking down the hallway in a blur.

"What the—?"

Shaking her head and smiling, she moved past him into the room. "That was Sam. My cat."

"You have a cat."

She shook her head at his disapproving tone. "You don't like them?"

"No."

"It's a good thing we weren't really married then." She kept her tone light. "I missed Sam a lot while I was gone."

"Sam."

"Samuel Adams."

He smiled then, causing another kind of tightness in her chest. "After the beer?"

She couldn't help but laugh. "No, after the patriot." Indicating her overstuffed, bright orange chair, she took the couch. "Have a seat."

Carefully he lowered his bulk, sinking into the soft cushions. "This thing makes it difficult to get up quickly—not a good thing for men in my line of work."

"You're not undercover any longer."

Again he went still, that particular kind of stillness that meant he was ten times more alert. "I shouldn't be disappointed." He considered her, a half smile playing across his lips. "But somehow I expected you'd welcome me with open arms once you found out I wasn't a criminal."

Open arms. As if. She shook her head. "You should have told me earlier. You know how I feel about lies."

His smile faded. "I couldn't. My partner's wife and daughter died because of a leak. I couldn't save them, only him and he nearly died, too."

"You still should have told me."

"I wasn't sure I could protect you from them. I brought the Claws down, Lyssa. But I wasn't able to save your sister."

Ignoring the sharp stab of hurt that came with his words, she sighed. "No one could save Claire. She destroyed herself."

"Like you want to?"

"What?" Shocked, she started to raise her hand to her mouth, clenching it into a fist instead. "How can you say that?"

"Easily. Trask told me you refuse to go to a safe house. You won't let me stay and help. So you must *want* the killer to get you."

"Of course not. That's stupid."

"Is it? This guy means business. You heard Trask—they think he'll try again. Do you understand? He'll try again. For you, Lyssa. You might not be so lucky next time. Let me help you. You're my wife."

"Wife?" She snorted. "Our marriage isn't real."

"It's real until one of us files for divorce. Have you?"

"You know I haven't." She squared her shoulders and lifted her chin. "If I file for divorce today, will you leave?"

For a moment he seemed at a loss for words. Cocky, confident Alex, who always found the right thing to say. He simply stared at her, his face blank. "No."

"I give up." She threw up her hands.

He didn't move. "What did they tell you about the UNSUB?"

Changing the subject. She recognized the tactic. Alex had always done that when she'd brought up something he hadn't wanted to discuss.

"Unknown subject," he elaborated. "Did they give you any information on how the serial killer operates?"

"It's been all over the news and in the paper." She closed her eyes, trying not to remember the stark terror she'd felt as the gloved hands closed around her throat. Terror Alex had supposedly felt as well.

Sighing, she rubbed the back of her neck, massaging the bruises her attacker's hands had left. Watching her, Alex seemed unaware that he mimicked her actions, as though he could feel the same brutal ache.

"Humor me." His expression dark, he flashed a grim smile. "I'm not going anywhere yet."

Yet. Another lure? She sighed again. "He's vicious and deranged. He's hunting young women, so far only here in the Catskills. And only at night, always from behind. He attacks like an animal, running, leaping on them, as though he were a cougar bringing down prey. Then he rips out their throats. You know all this."

"Yes. But you got away. How?"

"What saved me was my clumsiness. I tripped just as he launched himself at me. So he missed. I'd just taken—" Suddenly, perilously close to tears, she paused to regain control. Shock. Part of the aftermath of the attack.

"I'd taken a self-defense class." Finishing, she took one shuddering breath, then another. "I was able to keep him off me, though he managed to get his hands around my neck."

"Did you see him?"

"No. I told the police and the FBI the same thing. It was so dark. Cloudy, about to rain. There was no moon."

Though another tremor shook her, she kept her voice level. "It was so damn dark. He wore black. All I saw was the flash of his teeth. White teeth, abnormally sharp, like a vicious dog's."

Alex leaned forward. "The FBI thinks he has a large dog he uses to savage the bodies."

"But you don't."

"No." Though he kept his own hands at his sides, Lyssa could see they were clenched into fists. "I don't. I talked to Trask. He said I could look at the dossier they've made on him. I wanted to find you first."

This final lure did it. Though she knew reeling her in was his intention, this time she let him. Hook, line and sinker. "I want to look at this file." The more she knew about her enemy, the better prepared she'd be.

Alex nodded, as though to say he understood. The way he watched her reminded her yet again of a wild animal, studying prey. *Prey.* She shuddered.

"I'd like to turn the tables on this serial killer." She was unaware she'd spoken out loud until she saw Alex narrow his eyes. She lifted her chin.

"You would, would you?"

"I would. He needs to see what it feels like to be hunted."

"The FBI's all over this guy like fleas on a dog." Though he spoke nonchalantly, she sensed the tension underneath the casually spoken words.

"This is personal. They say he'll come after me again. Maybe I should turn the tables."

"Bad idea."

She shrugged. "Maybe. But I think it's worse to sit here and wait, like I'm bait or something."

"You'll need help."

Damn. He took her seriously. Did he realize that in itself was another, even more potent lure? "Help? Maybe."

"Then let me stay with you."

Lyssa pushed herself to her feet. Now she paced, feeling trapped. "There's no room. I don't have a guest room."

"So? I can sleep on the couch."

"I don't know…"

"I want this guy stopped."

She spun, facing him. "You really think we're going to be the ones to stop him?"

With the same careless smile she'd once found so devastatingly attractive, he had her. "Together we might."

Lyssa crossed her arms. Eagerness warred with exhaustion. "I don't know…"

"I want this guy." Fierce resolve colored his voice and shone from his caramel eyes. "I want him bad."

Violence rang in his voice. The elemental part of her thrilled to it. More stupidity. She shook off the feeling.

"The FBI is working on this. They're professionals."

"Yeah, and they don't like to share the glory. But I'm on leave from work and need something to do." His wicked smile widened. Whether he was joking or not, she couldn't tell.

"Lyssa, it's personal to me, too. He hurt you. Nobody hurts my mate and gets away with it."

At his words, she shivered. *His mate.* Though totally out of character, there was something primitive in the way he said it, something earthy that spoke to her inner soul.

Stupid. He was a fake husband, nothing more. Just because neither of them had filed the necessary paperwork to dissolve their union, didn't make it any more real. Still, she could use his help.

"You can stay," she snapped.

His entire face lit up, giving his rugged features the kind of masculine beauty that made her heart skip a beat. Doubly stupid. Memories of his mouth on her body, his tanned hands dark on her pale skin—no. She wasn't going there. "But not as my husband."

He moved his head in a solemn nod. "Of course not."

"On the couch."

Glancing at her bedroom door, a mere ten feet away, he nodded again. "Okay."

Decision made, she finally managed a genuine smile. Cramming her hands in her pockets, she stared at him hard. "Good. Now let's go talk to the FBI. I want to see that file."

"I thought you needed to get some rest."

While her body screamed for sleep, her mind had other ideas. "I can do that later."

She went to the door and yanked it open. "Are you

coming? You can drive. They've set up camp at the police station."

Alex made certain her guard on duty was alert and vigilant. Then, after making a quick call on his cell phone, they drove to the Wicket Hollow police station.

Trask met them at the door. One look at Lyssa, and he shook his head. "You didn't mention she was coming along."

Lyssa pushed past Alex to stand in front of the frowning agent. "I insisted."

His frown deepened. "You're a civilian. I can't let you see any of this. The press doesn't know a lot of the info in this folder. I'd like to keep it that way."

Alex opened his mouth. She stopped him with a wave of her hand. "Look, Agent Trask. Let's not do this. Don't make me fight to see what I should be entitled to know. Alex has offered to protect me. We both need whatever information you have."

If the agent found her choice of words odd, he didn't let on.

"Fine," Trask muttered. "I don't know why I even agreed to let you do this." He glared at Alex. "DEA isn't involved in this investigation."

Grinning, Alex stepped forward and clasped the other man's shoulder. "Professional courtesy?"

Trask raised an eyebrow and said nothing.

"All right. I don't know either." Alex flashed him a smile. Lyssa recognized the Alex she was coming to think of as the undercover Alex, the charming, carefree and confident one.

"But I appreciate it," Alex continued. "This guy attacked my wife."

The other man grunted and turned on his heel. They

followed him down the short hallway to a temporary war room. Charts and graphs had been tacked on the cracked, off-white walls. Manila file folders and stacks of computer printouts were spread over a long table and a desk. Half-empty coffee cups littered every surface. When they entered the room, a thin man with dark circles under his eyes looked up from his computer.

"Take a break, Tex," Trask ordered. "Go get some fresh coffee."

The young man knocked over his chair in his eagerness to obey. With a shy smile at Lyssa, he left the room.

"This is command central." Indicating the cluttered room, Trask pointed toward the front. A list was written on the chalkboard, with check marks to indicate which items had been worked. "Helps us keep track of things."

"Is it helping?"

"Not yet. Take a look at this." Trask handed Alex a thick, well-thumbed manila folder. "See what you make of it."

Pulling out a chair for her, Alex dropped into the one next to her and began to read. "So what do you think he does with the bones?"

Lyssa couldn't help but shiver. "He collects their bones?"

With a grimace, Trask tapped the chalkboard. "Bone, singular. Just one, a rib. That's why we call him the Bone Man."

Alex raised his head to look at her, his brown eyes intent. "The press doesn't know this," he cautioned. "They're still calling him the Catskill Killer."

She nodded to show she understood. "So he's collecting bones."

"Yeah. But first he rips out their throats. After they're dead, he takes his little souvenir."

She made an involuntary sound of revulsion. "That's strange. And awful."

"Nah." Trask wagged his finger at her. "That's really common among these guys, though his choice in itself is unusual. After he's let his dog—and the dog's a big one, judging from the size of the teeth marks—gnaw on the body awhile, he removes his rib and takes off."

Glancing at Alex, Lyssa took in his grim expression. She swallowed the bile that rose in her throat. "You already knew this?"

"Yeah. Trask briefed me the night of your attack."

She transferred her gaze to Trask. "So what do you think he's doing with the bones?"

"Some of the guys think he's making some sort of sculpture," Trask said. "Or using them in a ritual. Devil worship maybe."

A frown creasing his forehead, Alex cleared his throat. "What does your profiler think?"

"Trophies. Like all the others, he collects something so he can relive the obscene thrill the killing gave him."

None of this seemed to bother Alex as much as it did her. Trask either. Lyssa supposed this came with their line of work.

Another glance at Alex caught him again rubbing the back of his neck. She stopped herself from doing the same.

"Take a look." Trask pointed to a bulletin board where they had tacked pictures of all four of the previous victims. Lyssa saw her own photo off to the side.

Seeing all the women together made her chest hurt. Lyssa turned to Alex. "I knew they all looked the same—like me, but seeing them this way…"

Alex gave a curt nod. "I understand."

Trask tapped the board. "All tall, blond, and thin. All of them young—mid-twenties—and, with one notable exception, single."

"Me."

Both men looked at her.

"The one who got away." Trask didn't sound all that happy about it.

Lyssa shivered. "Why does that description sound so ominous? How much time do we have?"

"Before he acts again?" Trask glanced at a calendar. "The first two victims were killed roughly a month apart, on the night of the full moon. We believed we'd found a pattern until the third. No full moon."

"What about the fourth?"

"That's the thing. This guy's stepping up the intensity. The fourth victim was grabbed two weeks after the third."

"Then he went for Lyssa. No moon."

"Yeah." Trask frowned. "And only a week later. No pattern. We expect he'll attack again any day."

"And," Alex said, "though he stays in the Catskills, you have no idea where he'll strike next."

"Oh, but we think we do. According to Marty, our profiler, the UNSUB's still here in the area." Trask jerked his thumb at Lyssa. "Because of her. Maybe he doesn't know if she saw him. And she's his first failure. That's why she's under such heavy guard."

Lyssa made another sound, low in her throat. "Why?" She knew she let some of her impotent rage show in the single word, but didn't care. "And don't give me the standard 'he's insane' line. By now your people have developed a theory. I want to hear it."

Trask and Alex exchanged a look.

"She's good." Trask spoke grudgingly.

"Yes, she is." The coolness in Alex's voice contrasted with his wry smile.

"Marty thinks there's a reason to the Bone Man's madness. The large dog, the taking of the rib, the almost ritualistic way he arranges the bodies before he defiles them. It points to some sort of mythic belief, like the guy's trying to make himself into a super-hero or—" Trask shook his head, his expression dour "—a god."

Alex went still. Watching the intent way he listened while pretending nonchalance as he flipped through the file, she was positive he knew more than he was telling. No matter—as soon as she got him alone, she would make him share whatever information he was hiding.

"You finished?" Trask closed the folder and took it. "I could use a cup of coffee. How about you two?"

"Not now. Thanks." Distracted, this time Alex couldn't quite hide his growing agitation.

"What's wrong?" Trask eyed him. "Did you see something in the file we missed?"

"No." The too-short answer wasn't enough. Lyssa stared at Alex, willing him to go on. He stared back, then cleared his throat. "I need time to process this, to ana-lyze the threat and figure out the best way to neutralize it."

After a moment of startled silence, Trask chuckled, a dry, humorless sound. "No you don't. You're not on this case, remember? If you find out anything, anything at all, you're to come to me with it, understand?"

Alex's gaze slid past the man to the chalkboard and the nearly empty coffeepot. When he spoke again, he spoke so low he might have been talking to himself. "I often forget that I'm not undercover."

With a worried frown, Trask clapped him on the shoulder. "You need some R & R, buddy. After such a long undercover assignment, most guys would be on a beach somewhere, instead of jumping headfirst into the middle of something like this."

"Most guys," now Alex's voice rang out, determined and strong, "don't have a wife whose life is in danger. He shot the other man a wry look. "I've got to tell you, this guy makes me want to hunt him down and rip out his throat."

Lyssa nodded. How well she knew that feeling. When Claire had been murdered, she'd felt exactly the same. Still did, most days.

Trask's frown deepened. "Not good, man. You need to get that under control."

"Yeah. Not once in over ten years of law enforcement have I felt that way. Until now."

"You'd better go." Trask ran a hand through his spiky gray hair. "I've got a team meeting in ten minutes. If you come across any leads…"

"I'll keep you informed."

Lyssa rose when Alex did, striding down the hall ahead of him without another word. Once out into the bright spring sunshine, he took her arm.

She shook him off. "Don't. My skin's still crawling from those pictures."

"You've got to let them take you to a safe house."

"What?" She stopped short. "I left my home and my business more than three years ago, to try and save Claire. I just got back. I don't want to leave it again."

"You saw what he did to those women."

"Yes." She shivered, hunched in her coat, before squaring her shoulders. "It could have been me. But he missed. Now it's my turn."

"Your turn? How can I make you see?"

"You can start by telling me the truth. What did you figure out back there?"

Again he went still. "What do you mean?"

"I saw you. You read something that gave you a clue, but you didn't want to tell Trask. What was it?"

"Nothing. Like I said, I need to think about this."

She sighed. "Stubborn ass."

"Maybe. It's not over, Lyssa. Didn't you hear Trask? The profiler thinks this guy will come after you again."

"Him and what small army?" She gave a short, humorless laugh. "I'm well protected. He'll never get me now."

"You don't know what this guy is."

"And you do?"

He opened his mouth. Closed it. Said nothing.

"You won't tell me. Why?"

"Lyssa." He laid a hand on her shoulder. "Come on." Steering her toward his car, he sounded gruff. "Let's get back to the house."

The house. Suddenly she knew she couldn't go back there. Not yet. She dug in her heels. "First we need to go by the cemetery. I want to visit Claire."

"Have you lost your mind? Lyssa—"

"My sister's grave," she reiterated. "Please, Alex. I can't explain, but I need to do this before I go back under lock and key. You're with me. It's broad daylight. I'll be safe." Safe. Would she ever feel safe again?

He sighed. "Let me make a call. I'll need to let your guards know where we are."

He dialed, spoke a few words into his phone, and hung up. "All right." Still sounding doubtful, he opened the car door. "Let's go."

It was nearly noon when they arrived at Restful Wind Cemetery. As soon as he'd parked the car, Lyssa climbed up, letting him follow as she unerringly picked her way through the granite markers. The place felt quiet, as peaceful as the name promised. Since most of the trees were on the perimeter, they'd spot an intruder before he could get near them.

"She's over here." Lyssa glanced over her shoulder at him, then pointed. "I'll just be—"

She screamed.

Alex moved. Rushing to Lyssa, he grabbed her, pulling her close and trying to shield her from seeing. But he was too late. Way too late. She'd already seen.

Claire's grave had been defiled. What remained of her decomposed body had been scattered among the leaves and torn-up ground. Written in blood on the tombstone was a warning. *You're mine. King Nebeshed will rule again.*

Chapter 3

"Hounds and damnation." Alex's curse barely registered. Pushing herself away from him, Lyssa staggered backward, unable to look at him or the trampled, ruined ground, unable to look at anything. She gagged. Her stomach roiled and heaved. What little she'd been able to choke down that morning came up in a violent rush.

Alex turned away, giving her privacy. Silently she thanked him for that small kindness.

Hadn't she been through enough?

Claire. That bloody, shredded mess was all that remained of her baby sister.

"That's it," she gritted out. "I'm more than angry now. I'm royally, seriously pissed."

When she raised her head, Alex's expression looked cool, unreadable. "This is not Claire." He indicated the blood. "This is too fresh."

Wiping her mouth with her hand, she shuddered. "What do you mean?" She sounded hoarse, out of breath, like she'd been running hard. "What's not Claire?"

"The blood—he must have brought it with him." He grimaced, indicating the crimson splotches on the grass. "Some sort of sacrifice, maybe."

"Brought it with him? Why? How?"

"I don't know. But this is not from your sister." He softened his grim voice. "She's been dead too long."

While intellectually she knew that, even as she nodded she felt her gorge rise again. She swallowed, concentrating on deep breathing, slow and steady until she felt the nausea pass. In her purse she found some breath mints. Spearmint. She popped one in her mouth and focused on the burst of flavor.

Breathe in. Breathe out. She looked up at the sky—impossibly blue. Normal. Looked at the tops of the leafy green trees. Springtime. Pretty. Then she looked at the car. Alex's low-slung, black Corvette, parked at the curb.

She had to get out of here. Now. So she could think.

Fixing her gaze on the passenger door, she rolled her shoulders and lifted her head. Though she meant to stride, her steps were unsteady. But before she could reach out her hand to touch the shiny metal, Alex stepped in front of her and opened the door for her.

With a grateful nod, she slid into the seat, welcoming the cool feel of the leather. He closed the door behind her with a quiet thunk, then crossed around to the driver's side.

"Ready?"

Without meeting his gaze she nodded, keeping her head down and concentrating on her breathing. But despite the nausea, she had to ask, had to know.

"Where did the blood come from? You said a sacrifice. Did he—" she swallowed, reminding herself to breathe "—kill someone else?"

"Not someone. Something. An animal, most likely."

An animal. With a shuddering sigh, she swallowed back bile and popped another mint.

Alex started the car. The low rumble of the engine coming to life seemed soothing. As they pulled away from Restful Wind Cemetery, she closed her eyes and pretended to go to sleep, hoping to earn a few more moments of silence from her companion.

"We need to talk."

Not so lucky. Still, determined to give it one last shot, she kept her eyes screwed closed.

"Open your eyes. Sleeping is not an option right now."

Another flash of anger. Opening her eyes, she glared at him. "I'm not sleeping. But I can't, I don't—"

"Know how to deal with that?" A savage jerk of his fingers indicated the carnage they'd just left.

"Exactly."

"You're going to have to." Expression set in hard, grim lines, he stared back. "Lyssa, you've got to deal with it. We've got to deal with it. Who do you think that message was for?"

"Message?" Again she saw the bloody words, with their violent crimson trails down the smooth granite tombstone.

You're mine.

"Yes, message. The Bone Man meant that threat for you."

"No." She gave a bitter laugh. "King Nebeshed, whoever that may be, did that." To her dismay, her throat closed up. Defiantly, she cleared it.

"King Nebeshed is the Bone Man." If anything, he sounded more grim. "And the message was directed at you."

"Why Claire?" Anger and grief filled her eyes. She blinked away the scalding tears, fiercely determined not to cry. "She had nothing to do with him. She was dead long before he started his rampage."

Gently, so gently he made her chest ache, Alex put his hand on the back of her neck and massaged the tight knot there. "I'm thinking maybe Nemo really *didn't* kill your sister. He's claimed innocence all along."

She jerked away. "What are you saying?"

"It's possible this serial killer, this Bone Man, was the one. Even then, Claire fit his profile. She was tall and thin and blond, like you and the others. He might even have seen you with her. Maybe that's why he came after you."

Speechless, Lyssa could only twist her hands in her lap, over and over. Again fury rose in her, chasing away all other emotion.

When she spoke, her voice vibrated with her anger. "Why would you say that? Why would you even think it? Nemo killed my sister. Claire was Nemo's woman. You know he thought he owned her."

"We have no proof." He spoke gently. "And even if we did, he didn't do this. He's locked up, behind bars."

"Are you sure he hasn't escaped?"

"I'd know if he had. He's still in prison."

"You seriously believe that Claire might have been—"

"The Bone Man's first victim? Now that I've seen the warning, yes, I do."

Numb, she shook her head. "But he didn't take a bone from Claire."

"Maybe he did—no one checked. She was pretty torn up when she was killed."

"Why defile her grave now?" Again she saw the scene. Smelled the copper scent of the blood. So much blood.

"As a warning to you. He wants you now."

"So you're saying this guy was around then, when I was trying to get Claire out of Hades Claws?"

"You never know."

An answer that wasn't an answer. Though what did she expect? This was Alex, the master of disguise.

"Who is he then? One of Hades Claws? There were so many of them. I know the entire gang didn't go to jail. So how do we know which one is him?"

"I need to talk to Trask." He punched a number into his cell phone. Low-voiced, he spoke for a moment, filling in Trask on the scene at the cemetery.

Disconnecting, he replaced the phone in his belt clip and looked at her. The expression in his eyes made her shiver.

"Trask said the FBI will notify the local police. This guy's out to get you, Lyssa. You. The Bone Man knows you visit Claire's grave. He expected you. Those words, that blood, that was a warning to you."

Even as she shook her head in denial, she knew he was right. She fingered the bruises on her throat. Somehow, someway, this deranged serial killer had left his mark on her. Claimed her. Now he wanted to make sure she knew it.

"Who's King Nebeshed?"

Alex looked away. "I don't know."

Though she thought he might be lying yet again, this time she let it go. For now. "Is he playing with me, toying with me before he—"

"Moves in for the kill? I think so."

"Why? He didn't do this to the others."

"Who knows? Maybe he thinks he owns you."

Her thoughts of a moment ago. Wincing, she forced herself to lift her chin, displaying the yellow-and-purple bruises her attacker had given her. "He's got a fight on his hands then."

Alex frowned. "You don't mean to go after him."

"I'll defend myself. I can, you know."

"Not alone. Not against him. You don't know what he is."

"Again I ask—and you do?"

At her sharp retort he looked away, before swinging his head back to look hard into her eyes. "Yes."

His succinct answer sent a chill up her spine. "How?"

As he opened his mouth to answer her, his cell phone rang.

"Lupe." After identifying himself, Alex listened. He cursed, then closed the flip-phone with a snap.

Something in the way he looked at her...

"What is it? What's happened?"

He grimaced. "There's been a break-in at your house."

"Just now?" She couldn't believe it. "What about the guards, the police? Surely they're still there."

"That's what makes this even worse. Whoever broke into your place did it right under their noses. In broad daylight. No one left their post."

She closed her eyes, momentarily disoriented.

"What if you'd been inside? Alone? We've got to get you out of here, Lyssa. They have a safe house ready. Say the word and I'll take you there."

Safe. She hadn't felt safe in years. Not since Claire had begun using drugs. "That simple, huh?"

He caught the note of sarcasm in her voice and raised a brow. "Do you have a death wish? Is that it?"

She thought of her nursery, of the simple pleasures she'd found in the rich smell of damp earth, in her green, growing plants eagerly stretching for the sun. Of Sam's throaty purr as she'd stroked his fur with her fingers. Small things like that had kept her going since she'd lost her sister. "No. That's not it at all. I don't want to die."

"Then why won't you go where we can keep you safe?"

"If he murdered my sister the same way he's destroyed those other women, then I want him." She flexed her fingers, knowing he would think she was foolish and not caring. "He's mine, Alex. Mine."

"You want revenge." His flat tone told her his thoughts about that.

"Maybe." She considered, then decided to throw caution to the winds. "Yes. I do. I want revenge. He tried to kill me once, and failed. If he's the one who did that to Claire—"

"He's not your everyday, average criminal."

"I didn't think he was."

"He's a killer. A serial killer. Do you understand what that means?" The harshness in his tone took her aback, before she realized he was only trying to protect her.

"I think I do."

He slowed and turned. Surprised, she realized they were in her driveway. Home, already. Along with four police cars, two of them state, and several other unmarked sedans parked on both sides of the street.

"What the—?"

"They're investigating the break-in."

"Did he take anything?" The thought of her personal belongings in the hands of that murderer turned her stomach.

"They don't think so."

Puzzled, she frowned. "Then what did he want?"

"You, Lyssa. He wanted you. And when he didn't find you…"

Oh, God. She closed her eyes and took a deep breath. Opening them, she forced herself to meet Alex's gaze. "He trashed the place, didn't he?"

"You could call it that." Grim-voiced, he indicated the swarm of uniforms. "I've asked them to beef up your security."

She nodded, pushed herself up from the low-slung seat. "I'm sure that'll be enough."

"I'm not."

His terse response made her give him a tired smile. "The Bone Man *is* human, you know."

Meeting her gaze, he didn't smile back. "I wouldn't be too sure about that," he said.

"You're right." She nodded. "Maybe *inhuman* would be a better word."

Alex didn't reply.

Together, they went into the house.

Hours later. Question after question after question. Cradling a traumatized Samuel Adams in her arms, Lyssa let her head sag against the back of her once-overstuffed couch. Hyperaware of Alex standing nearby, one arm propped against the wall near the doorway, she made a point out of keeping her chin up. Through all the questioning, he'd remained there, silently watching, making her feel as if she had her own

personal bodyguard in the man the others kept refer-
ring to as her husband.

Her husband. What a stretch. No, not really, not if she
remembered to insert the word *temporary* before *husband.* Her temporary husband. Who must, for some reason known only to himself, feel responsible for her.
He'd made that crystal clear. Shown by his brief appearance at Claire's funeral, duty propelled him. He wasn't
here because she'd haunted him the way he'd haunted
her.

She wasn't sure how she felt about that. For now, because the horror of her sister's violently disturbed grave
site combined with the utter destruction of most of her
personal belongings overwhelmed her, she couldn't
think about it. This latest assault seemed nearly as in-
vasive as the first, as if the Bone Man had violated her
by pawing through her home before wrecking it.

And *wrecking* didn't even begin to describe what
he'd done. Torn cushions, shredded sheets, rugs, tow-
els. The place looked like a large, angry beast had been
let loose inside, to wreak havoc on anything not made
of steel. She couldn't look anywhere—not even at the
pictures that had once hung on her walls—without seeing his mark.

Worst of all was the blood.

Like Claire's grave site, blood had been flung all
over everything. Splatters of crimson, rivulets of scarlet, the promise of violence was everywhere. Here, in
the close confines of her small home, she could smell
even more the awful, coppery scent of it, making her
stomach roil and toss again.

But in one thing she'd been lucky. Somehow Samuel Adams had escaped the killer's notice. She'd found

her pet hiding in the back of her closet, hunkered down behind her clothes, clearly traumatized. He'd allowed her to remove him and hold him, but his trembling hadn't abated until a few minutes ago.

Stroking her cat's soft fur had kept her from losing it. Holding Sam, she'd perched on the edge of her ripped sofa and tried to coherently answer the FBI's questions. No, she hadn't left any windows unlocked. Yes, the only unsecured port of entry was her cat door, much too small for any human to enter through. Finally, the FBI finished their questioning. Snapping the notepad closed, Trask glanced at Alex.

"You staying here?"

Alex pushed himself away from the wall and jerked his head in a nod. "For now." He shot a glance at Lyssa. "At least until I can convince her to go someplace else."

"We've got a man in front and one in back."

"Locals or—"

"Locals. I've asked for some extra men but they can't spare the manpower."

"Not enough." Alex frowned. "This guy's smart, he's fast, and he wants her bad."

"I'm working on it."

"The guy got past them once. Go higher up. Get some good shooters out here."

With a grimace, Trask conceded the point. "I'll leave one of my own men. In a supervisory capacity."

"I want two men. In a guarding capacity. Give me the best you've got."

To Lyssa's amazement, Trask didn't even hesitate. With a grim smile, the FBI agent clapped Alex on the shoulder. "Fine. You've got them."

"Thanks." He walked the other man to the door. When Trask had gone, Alex came back to stand next to the couch.

"You should try and get some rest." His voice was oddly gentle, a marked change from the harsh way he'd barked out orders to Trask.

She lifted her chin. "You're not in charge of me, despite the way Trask let you tell him what to do."

He narrowed his eyes. "Only because what I asked for made sense. And I'm not trying to tell you what to do. You mentioned earlier how badly you need to rest."

"I can't." Forcing herself to relax, she gave a deliberately casual shrug. "Every time I close my eyes, I see my sister's grave." She swallowed, unable to continue, breathing slowly and steadily through her nose.

He nodded. The intensity of his stare made her turn away. "Have you thought about what I said?"

"About the safe house?"

"Yes."

"I have to clean up here." She glanced around, then winced. "Look at this place."

Alex jammed his hands in his pockets. "Come on, Lyssa. You can't stay here. It's not safe. First the grave site, then this. He's too close. And he's staking his claim. After all, he tried for you once and failed."

Barely. She thought of that night. Felt the hands, so large, so insanely powerful, around her throat, squeezing the life from her. The classes in self-defense had not prepared her for the shock of a real attack. All of her training had flown out the window.

The Bone Man had come closer to winning than he knew. Than anyone knew. She'd have to get a hell of a lot better if she was going to go up against him.

She shook her head. Blinked. "I'm safe now. I have a guard. Two police, two FBI agents and you."

"Not enough. The house was guarded and he got inside anyway. Let them put you in a safe house."

"It wouldn't change anything. He'd find me there too, just like he found me here."

Alex made a sound. Frustration or anger, which she didn't know. "This guy's not psychic."

"He found me here, didn't he? If he was the one that killed Claire, he knew where I went after Hades Claws. And you tried to keep that quiet, didn't you?"

Alex narrowed his eyes. "I buried the information. Even Carson, my best friend, couldn't find you."

"Then how…"

"I don't know."

Saying those words cost him, she could tell. "Have you thought it might be revenge against you? For bringing them down?"

"These attacks weren't against me."

"But they—he—thinks I'm your wife."

He cursed. "I don't think that's the reason. If he wanted revenge, if he wanted to make me suffer, he'd have gone for you first. But he attacked four others before you, five if you count Claire. He's been looking for someone all along. Now he appears convinced you might be the one."

"Why?"

"Who knows. He's insane."

Fighting the urge to pace, she clenched her hands into fists. "Fair enough. But assuming your theory is correct and the Bone Man wanted me but killed Claire, does the FBI agree with you that she could have been his first victim?"

He nodded.

"Pretty tidy," she mocked. "You think you've got this guy and his motives all wrapped up, don't you?"

"Don't make it more complicated than it is. The Bone Man wants you. He's enjoying the hunt."

She studied him, unable to read much in his shuttered expression. "You understand him?"

He shrugged. "Sort of. So far he's been pretty much a textbook case. The profilers have him pegged. Or think they do."

Again that tone…

"Are the profilers always right?"

"Most of the time, yes." He squinted, glanced down at his hands. "But I don't think they're on target this time."

"You think you know better?"

"Maybe." Moving so suddenly that she had no time to react, he gripped her shoulders. "Lyssa, listen to me. This isn't a game."

She refused to back away, even though his face, his beautiful, sensual mouth, was mere inches from her own.

"So you've said, many times. Don't try to intimidate me, Alex."

He came closer. So close that his breath stirred her hair, so close that his mouth hovered over hers.

"Intimidate?" His voice might have been a growl. "Is that what you think I'm trying to do?"

A rush of yearning filled her. How simple a thing, how easy it would be, to simply lean forward and touch her lips to his, to lose herself in the sensuality promised by his mouth. One touch and she knew what would happen. They'd gone up in flames together before.

No. Those nights were another thing she couldn't allow herself to think about. She certainly didn't want— or need—a repeat.

He breathed. She wavered. Then she forced herself to turn her head. "Intimidation is a bad idea." Her voice sounded blessedly normal.

"Do you really think I'm trying to intimidate you?"

"Aren't you?"

"No. I want you to be safe." Alex glared down at her, making her aware again of how large he was. Large and solid and male. "If you think I could simply run out on you now, when you've got this deranged murderer after you, then you have no idea what kind of man I am." He shook his head, the heat in his eyes searing her like a touch. "I take my responsibilities seriously."

Responsibility. Duty. Why wasn't she entirely comfortable with that?

She held herself stiffly, uncomfortably aware of his closeness but unwilling to be the one to move away. His masculine scent, the faint whiff of soap and outdoors, assaulted her senses. One more time, she vowed silently, she'd make one more attempt to set him free from his imagined responsibility to her. After that he was on his own.

She tilted her head, steeling herself to meet his gaze dead on. "Alex, for the last time you don't—"

"I know I don't have to. I'm here because I want to. I want to be here for you," he said. The words didn't sound trite, coming from him. Especially coming from him, even though she knew his sense of duty colored every word.

She tried to reply, wanting sarcasm, to tell him she didn't need his help, but couldn't push a sound from her too-tight throat. All her life, she'd always been there for someone else. First for her mother when her father had run out, then for her sister after their mother had died. No one, not once in her life, had ever offered to be there for her. Until now.

And despite the fact that she didn't want or need any help, despite the fact that her life was just fine as it was—or at least as it had been before Claire had gotten herself killed, his words touched something deep inside her.

The grave, the blood…all at once, what had happened came rushing back at her and she swayed on her feet. To her furious disbelief, her eyes filled with tears. She blinked, then, accepting them, she let them run silently down her face while she stood there pretending none of this mattered.

He cursed and she stiffened.

"Let me take you away," he said, his tone level. Reasonable. "You and me. No one else. I swear I'll protect you."

Slowly she raised her head. "No safe house?"

"No."

"But—"

"You *will* be safe." He uttered the promise like a vow.

"Will you train me to protect myself?"

He stared at her. "What?"

"I want to learn. I took that self-defense class, but it wasn't enough. I want you to show me as much as you can."

"What are you planning?"

She shook her head. "To defend myself. Teach me how to shoot a gun."

For a moment he continued to watch her, his expression shuttered. Then he nodded. "I will."

Oddly enough, his promise was enough to decide her. "Will the FBI let you do this?"

"Screw the FBI. I protect what is mine."

The force of his words made her smile. She thought about arguing the fact that she belonged to no one, and discarded it. Such trivial distinctions mattered little in a battle over life and death.

"All right, I'll go with you." She made her decision quickly, knowing if she thought much more about it she'd drive herself crazy. "When do you want to leave?"

He waited until she looked him full in the face, locking her in with the intensity of his gaze. Some odd sort of primitive power blazed from him, making her catch her breath and wonder if the nonsense he'd claimed about a connection between them might possibly be true.

"Now."

Chapter 4

"Now?" She moved away, shaking off his hand. He watched her as she began to pace, willing her to understand the urgency now that she'd made her decision.

Lyssa. He found her fierceness pleasing, even though her determination to fight back scared the hell out of him. The contradiction of her willowy frame and strength intrigued him. The sight of her silent tears had caused a peculiar hitch in his chest. He had zero experience with weeping women—after all, he'd only seen his sister, Brenna, cry once in her entire life—but he had an inkling most women were much more noisy about it than Lyssa. She'd gone soft, just once letting go of the steel backbone that he was learning supported her in everything she did.

He forced himself to concentrate on the matter at hand—keeping her safe. The reference to King Nebeshed had clinched it for him. "We need to go at once, while we still have the element of surprise."

"How?" Looking away, she sounded curt. "They'll never let us leave. They think they're protecting me. Trask said they were going to beef up surveillance."

"Twenty-four/seven." Surprised his voice sounded normal, Alex watched her as she resumed her pacing. "But they trust me. I'm one of them."

Back and forth, her long-legged stride graceful, pivoting as she turned, fluid and certain. Like a wolf. Like his mate.

He thought longingly of *change,* that moment when he could lose his human form and abandon himself to the wild. He couldn't now, but he must do so soon. His very nature insisted. Would Lyssa understand?

And, if the Bone Man was what Alex thought he was, the upcoming battle would demand it.

Still pacing, Lyssa muttered under her breath.

As though none of this mattered, he resumed his pose leaning against her wall with his shoulder, arms crossed as if they had all the time in the world.

She stopped dead in her tracks and nailed him with a look. "Stop that."

"Stop what?"

"Watching me like you'd like to devour me."

The hunger that had been simmering in him rose to a near boil. He let his nostrils flare; the only sign that he was close to losing control. "Maybe I would."

She stepped back, her hand going to her hair in a defensive gesture. "Alex, there's something we should get straight between us."

Raising a brow, he waited.

"If we're going to go away together, I can't have you

trying to seduce me. I've got enough problems right now without having to deal with that."

Puzzled, he narrowed his eyes. "I haven't tried to seduce you."

"No. I know." Color stained her cheeks. "But I remember the weekend of Claire's funeral."

"I started out to comfort you."

"I know." She looked him full in the face. "But our chemistry took over. We've always had that between us. Now, even your presence is a sort of seduction, Alex. Surely you realize that."

Would she never cease to surprise him? Mulling over this piece of information, he watched her.

"No, I didn't." He smiled, amused despite of—or maybe because of—her confusion. He couldn't resist teasing her. "But that is good to know. I'll have to keep it in mind."

"No." She smiled herself, a tentative thing that brought her an aching sort of beauty. "I—we—don't need any distractions. We need to concentrate on making sure this guy is caught."

Giving himself a mental shake, he nodded. "You're right. We need to concentrate on that. On making sure you aren't—"

"His next victim."

"Right." He considered her. "Agreed. Now, let's go out a back window."

"What?" She gaped at him. Then, visibly collecting herself, she shook her head. "That won't work. They're guarding the outside too."

He waved that worry away. "Small-town cops. They have no idea. I guarantee you they won't catch us."

"There's FBI. Trask's men."

"They'll be watching for someone coming in, not someone trying to leave."

"I don't know…"

His stomach rumbled, reminding him he hadn't eaten. "Okay, then we'll say we're going out for lunch."

"They'll want to go with us. For protection."

"Not if I tell them not to." He knew he sounded arrogant, but didn't care. "Your choice. We sneak out or we lie. But we need to do it now."

"I couldn't possibly eat." She raised a hand to her abdomen. "Not after…that."

As if on cue, his stomach growled again, much louder this time. "I could. I need to. And, it's a convenient excuse to leave."

She caught her lower lip between her teeth. "They'll want to order a pizza. Tony's here in town makes fantastic pies. They all know that."

Pizza? He needed red meat. Lots of it.

"Not pizza. Steak maybe. At the very least, a thick, juicy burger." He glanced at his watch, then the door. "Pack what you need," he told her. "Then decide."

She swallowed, looking ill. "I need to find Sam."

"Damn. Do you have to bring the cat?"

She glared at him. "I'm not leaving him here."

"Fine. Get him and let's go."

"Give me a minute."

He tapped his watch. "You've got it. Window or out to eat?"

With a sigh, she glanced at her darkened bedroom. "Window. My room is at the back of the house."

"Let's do it. Go get your cat."

Still she prevaricated. "Are you sure it's safe?"

"You're with me."

She grimaced. "You didn't answer my question."

He waited until he had her full attention, wanting her to know he was determined. "I'll keep you safe, Lyssa."

Staring back, she nodded, then hurried away to pack her things.

Though he'd just come close to speaking one of the most solemn oaths of his people, she didn't know that. Of necessity, he'd left off the final part of the vow—the word *always*.

He couldn't promise her always. Not without her knowing the truth about him—about what he was. He'd keep her safe. No more, no less.

A few minutes later, she emerged from her bedroom.

"Ready?" He sounded curt. She nodded, brushing past him with a large tote bag he figured she'd packed with clothes. The bag let out a disgruntled *mrrr-ow*.

Alex raised a brow.

"He doesn't like closed-in spaces." Head held high, she glanced from Alex to the closed front door to the bedroom with its single window. "Are you ready?"

Still eyeing her bag, Alex nodded. He hoped his expression made it plain he had grave doubts as to the wisdom of her decision to bring her cat.

"Sam's my fur-faced child," she said. Reaching into her bag, she stroked her cat's fur. "He's growling right now, showing his displeasure, but he'll settle down on top of my favorite T-shirt in a minute. When he does, he'll begin purring."

Cats. "Come on." Glaring at her bag, Alex stalked to the bedroom. Her bed was unmade, the bright colored comforter in tangles over the soft, cotton sheets. He couldn't help but remember the last time he'd been in this bed, with her wrapped up in his arms.

"Alex." Sharp-voiced, Lyssa's reprimand told him she knew his thoughts. Again.

He crossed to the window. It opened easily enough. He held up a finger, silently keeping her back while he slipped through and checked the perimeter. Clear. "Some guard," he muttered. "The FBI should know better than to rely on locals, manpower shortage or not."

Going back, he held out his hand.

Sliding her fingers into his, Lyssa appeared to be concentrating on making a graceful exit. With the heavy cat tote bag over one shoulder, she swung one leg up and out, dividing her balance between that foot and Alex's support of her hand.

Once her feet hit the ground, he suppressed the urge to give her a little tug and pull her up against him.

Still undetected, they kept to the bushes that skirted the driveway, reaching the 'vette without incident.

Keeping the tote in her lap while she slid into the seat, as soon as the door closed, Lyssa hurriedly unzipped the top. Shaking his ears, Sam poked his head up, making a low-throated sound.

Recognizing the sound, Alex narrowed his eyes. "Is he growling at me now?"

She nodded, stroking her pet's soft fur. "Can you blame him? You aren't exactly friendly toward him."

"I've never been one for cats." He turned the key. The powerful engine roared to life. "They're bound to hear this. Get ready."

Shifting into drive, he gunned the gas. The car shot forward.

Sam yowled.

Alex flashed a savage grin. "No pursuit yet." He turned right at Maple, the first cross street. Then left on

Forty-second. Only when they'd navigated a twisted maze of back roads did he slow the car to a reasonable speed.

Still stroking her pet, Lyssa glanced over her shoulder. "Some protectors."

"I know." He drummed his fingers on the steering wheel. "Lyssa, I want you to promise me something."

"What?"

"If I teach you how to shoot a gun, that doesn't make you an instant expert. Promise me—no crazy stunts, no attempts at revenge."

She stared. "I'm not stupid. I know I can't go it alone."

"This guy's not your average serial killer."

"Is there even such a thing?"

He made a sound of exasperation. "You know what I mean. The Bone Man is not someone who will make it easy to take him down."

Again, unease prickled along her spine. "You talk like you know him."

Know him? The reference to King Nebeshed had told him the truth. The serial killer didn't have a dog, he'd bet his life on that. This murderer, this crazed criminal who'd attacked Lyssa, was a shape-shifter. His own kind. But a shape-shifter run amok, much like the were-wolves of old.

King Nebeshed, the dark man. Looking for his consort, the woman of light.

Alex remembered the old story from his childhood. The dark man of legend had been a shape-shifter. A darkly evil king, who had ruled with a bloody hand. He'd taken as wife a human woman, a witch who was immortal as long as she was faithful to him. The tale said that, as a test, the dark man would kill her. No matter how many times he poisoned her or ripped off her head, she would reawaken the next morning, vibrant and full of life, while his power increased tenfold.

If this killer believed he was the dark man of legend, come to life, he would kill until he found his immortal mate. Impossible. And when the FBI finally caught up with him, by his actions he would take down the carefully constructed screen that normal members of the Pack had spent centuries building with their councils and their laws.

All shape-shifters were governed by their "Packs," in a manner similar to the U.S. government. Most shifters belonged to local Packs, which might be city or county, depending on the area. All were more loosely governed by state Packs and, instead of one giant, national Pack, the country was split into three regions—East, Central and West

If what Alex believed was true, the threat was far greater than he'd originally believed. Not only was the threat against Lyssa, but against his entire race. By one of his own kind. An insane freak. This made the killer ten times more dangerous. The Bone Man would destroy an entire way of life, returning the shape-shifters to days of being feared and hunted by humans.

Alex would need to contact the Pack Elders, the council. Ordinary police could never protect against one so powerful. As for Lyssa, he would have to decide quickly how much of the truth she should know. Revealing himself to her was a big risk—one he wasn't certain he should take.

Alex wanted to growl himself. He was tired of the lie, of keeping one eye open. He felt like he was always undercover, though instead of portraying a drug dealer slash biker, he was pretending to be human.

"Alex?" Lyssa's voice brought him back to the present. "I said, you talk as if you know him."

He said the first thing that came to mind. "I'm DEA."

"So? Since when does the drug enforcement agency deal with serial killers?"

Shaking his head, he didn't reply. They drove for a moment in silence; the low thrum of the Corvette's motor combined with Sam's purring to make an oddly soothing sound. Beside him, Lyssa almost relaxed. Almost. But he could tell, something still bothered her. Like him, she'd learned to trust her instincts.

"What kind of man are you?"

One corner of his mouth quirked. "A little late to ask me that, isn't it?"

"I'm serious." As though sensing her unease, Sam m-rowled. Stretching, he kneaded her T-shirt with his paws, glaring up at Alex, ears back.

Distracted, Lyssa resumed stroking her pet, threading her fingers through his soft fur until he began to relax.

Still, the cat and Alex eyed each other, Alex glancing from the road to the cat and back again.

Lyssa sighed. "You really don't like cats, do you?"

"Not particularly."

"Sam doesn't realize he's a cat. He thinks he's human."

Alex gave a dry chuckle. "Don't we all?"

"What an odd thing to say."

"Not really." His stomach growled again. "You know, I do need to get something to eat."

"I can tell." She wrinkled her nose. "If you keep

going on this road, there's a place about half a mile outside of town, right before you hit the interstate."

"Do they have steak?"

"I hear they have killer hamburgers." She sighed. "And great salads, though nausea has effectively eliminated what little appetite I might have had."

"That'll have to do."

As they pulled into the parking lot, her cat continued to regard Alex with loathing.

"Friendly cat." He smiled to take the sting off his words.

"I've never seen Sam like this. I don't know what's wrong with him. He likes most people."

"I'm not like most people." Alex stabbed a button to lower his window. They were one car away from the drive-through speaker.

"Do you want anything?"

She started to shake her head no, but glanced down at her pet. "A small hamburger, please."

Interpreting the gesture, Alex snorted. "For the cat?"

"He likes an occasional treat."

"What about you? Do you want a burger?"

"Not a burger. A salad maybe."

"A salad won't fill you up. You need meat. Protein."

"Alex, I'm a vegetarian."

"You're *what?*" She'd succeeded in shocking him. Alex, who had long ago considered himself past being shocked about anything, stared at her with his mouth open.

Lyssa laughed, the first genuine sound of amusement he'd heard her make in a while. "You can pull forward." She pointed to the departing car ahead of them. "And place your order."

He didn't move. "You're a what?"

"I don't eat meat."

Still glaring at Alex, Sam gave a kitty-growl.

"When did this start?"

"A little while ago. I just don't like meat any more."

Behind them, someone honked. Alex pulled the car forward. He barked his order into the speaker. "Two large hamburgers, one small. A large order of fries. Two Diet Cokes. And—" he glanced at Lyssa, still frowning "—a dinner salad, with ranch dressing."

As the cashier confirmed his order and gave him the total, he glanced at Lyssa to gage her reaction.

She smiled. "How'd you know I like ranch dressing?"

"I remember. Eating all those salads, I always thought you were dieting. I can't believe I didn't notice you didn't eat meat period."

"I was dieting. But Claire was a vegetarian. I decided to try it after…." She cleared her throat. "She would have enjoyed your reaction." Lyssa's smile widened.

"Why?" He handed his money to the cashier, accepting a grease-stained bag in return. Handing Lyssa her soft drink, he closed his window and pulled forward, into a parking spot.

"Claire liked shocking people."

Stabbing his straw into the plastic top of his drink, he grimaced. "So did most of the Hades Claws."

His terse reply must have reminded her again of things she'd been trying to forget. Her smile vanished, and the light disappeared from her face. Damn it.

"Sorry. I didn't mean to bring that up. That's been my life for the last couple of years, so—"

"You don't have to explain." She handed him his

first burger, then the fries. "I'm trying to learn to deal with losing my sister. Or I was, until he defiled her grave."

Sam m-rowled. Alex scowled at him before returning his attention to his burger. It was well done. He preferred rare. But these days he couldn't get any place to cook hamburger the way he liked it.

"Don't worry, Sam." Lyssa fished the smaller burger from the bag. "I've got yours." Unwrapping it, she broke off a chunk and held it out to her pet.

Delicately, Sam sniffed. Then, apparently finding the morsel acceptable, he ate it in two bites and mewed. Whether approval or thanks, Alex couldn't tell. But then, he didn't speak cat.

Signaling, Alex made a left turn, picking up speed as they entered the interstate. Though he tried to be casual about it, he knew Lyssa noticed him checking the rearview mirror.

Finally, she glanced over her shoulder. "What?"

"No tail."

"That's good." She fed Sam another morsel. "I love the feel of his soft sandpaper tongue licking my fingers."

Alex watched her, trying not to remember what else she liked the feel of. In their short time together, he'd learned a lot about Lyssa's sensual nature.

Finishing his first burger, he reached for his second. Lyssa finally retrieved her salad and opened it, picking at the lettuce with her fork. She caught him watching her and wrinkled her nose at him, making him chuckle. Glad she no longer regarded him like something the cat had dragged in, he couldn't help but wonder how she would regard him if he showed her his true self. If he changed to a wolf in front of her, would she run screaming from him in horror? Or would she somehow be able to understand?

Understanding—both of him and of their enemy—might be all that kept her alive. He glanced at her, then back at the road, and he knew. He had no choice. He'd have to show her, and the sooner the better. The only question was—how?

When Alex fell silent, Lyssa let her head rest against the back of the smooth leather seat. "Are you going to tell me where we're going or make me pry it out of you?"

He cocked his head, his expression serious. "Lyssa, I think I've figured out something about the Bone Man. I've got to show you something."

Everything about the way he spoke—his dark tone, the inflection in his voice—sounded like a warning. She shivered. Sam huffed, batting his paw in Alex's general direction like swatting a gnat.

"Show me what?"

He glanced back over his shoulder then took the next exit without signaling. The rural two-lane curved sharply and he took it at a too-fast speed. Lyssa clutched the door handle with one hand, her tote bag and Sam with the other.

Still grim-faced, Alex turned right onto a rutted gravel road.

A prickle of unease made her shiver again. Sam sensed something, too. Though she continued to stroke him, the cat's ears were flat against his head. Then he hissed, something he only did rarely, in extreme situations.

"You're scaring my cat."

"I'm sorry." His expression unreadable, he alternated

his attention between her and the potholes in the road. "I know you've been through a lot, Lyssa. There's more, but better you should learn this from me than him."

"Now you're scaring the hell out of me, not just Sam."

Jerking the steering wheel to the right, Alex pulled off the deserted road, onto a rutted track that went into the woods. Tall trees formed a canopy overhead, blocking out the sun and the sky. Once the main road vanished around a curve, he stopped the car.

She looked at him.

He looked at her. His hard expression momentarily softened. "I've got to do something that might seem—" he swallowed "—*will* seem strange. Please don't be afraid. I'm not going to hurt you, I promise."

"What a weird thing to say."

"Yeah." He looked away, then back at her. "This is important to me, necessary. You have to know…"

"Know what?"

His jaw worked. "You'll see in a minute. Trust me, okay?"

Hesitating only slightly, she dipped her chin in a nod. "I left with you, didn't I?"

"Yes. But this is…different. What I'm going to do will seem really bizarre to you, but I wouldn't do it if I didn't feel I had to."

"You're scaring the hell out of me."

"I know—I can already feel your tension." He stared at her.

Her heart began to pound. She licked her lips.

"I'm sorry," he muttered. "Before I change, I've got to do this." Leaning across the seat, he covered her mouth with his.

Tasting, branding, *claiming*. Alex. Her Alex. Deepening the kiss, exploring and touching and caressing.

Lyssa began to melt. Kissing him back, she wound her arms around his neck. Senses on overload, reeling, her desire spiraled. Warm—too hot—too many clothes. Her breasts ached for his hands to cup them, her nipples hardened as she pressed herself against his chest. More—she wanted more.

Finally, just as she was on the verge of peeling off her T-shirt, he broke away. Mortified, she felt heat color her face.

His chest rose and fell as he breathed as hard and fast and furious as her. Eyes dark, he looked at her. "It's time."

Bemused, she inhaled. "Time?"

"I have to show you now." He looked away, his jaw set. "Hold on to your cat—and Lyssa?"

Unable to answer, she simply stared at him.

"Please remember I would *never* hurt you. No matter what you see, remember that."

Was he into violent sex? Rape fantasies? No, not the Alex she knew from the past. Then what—?

One hand on the door handle, he turned and studied her again. "Afterward, promise you'll let me explain."

"Explain what? I can't promise anything when I don't know what you mean. Give me a break, Alex. I've been through a lot."

"You're a strong woman." He spoke as though proud of her. "You won't run screaming." He pushed open his door and unfolded himself from his seat. As he walked around the front of the car, she kept a firm hold on Sam's collar, her pulse skittering despite his assurances.

Twenty feet from the car, he stopped. Half turning,

he slipped off his shoes, then socks, placing them neatly beside him. His T-shirt went next. Lyssa watched in open-mouthed fascination as he pulled it over his head. His chest looked exactly as she remembered, all tight, corded muscles and rippling pecs.

When he started on his belt buckle, her amazement gave way to nervous anticipation. Expression serious, he turned his back to her, giving her a great view of his tight rear as he stepped out of his jeans.

Then he stood, still facing away from her in all his naked glory, and raised his face to the leafy treetops and slice of blue sky.

A shiver of longing and something else—warning?—rippled along her skin. What now? What was next?

In her lap, Sam tensed. With a light touch, she soothed him, focused on Alex.

As she watched, the air—or Alex—shimmered. His form wavered as he lifted his muscular arms. She caught her breath. He looked primitive, beautiful, like some handpicked, mythical supplicant beseeching the gods of old. Still swollen from his kiss, her lips tingled. Desire, long suppressed, quickened her pulse.

Alex.

Prickles of light stabbed the air, so bright she shaded her eyes. Alex stepped forward, away from her. The space around him swirled, he crouched low to the ground and—his shape changed.

A huge silver wolf stood where Alex had been.

Lyssa rubbed her eyes, certain she wasn't seeing properly. "What the—?"

Sam hissed, arching his back and digging his claws into her arm through the bag. He growled, low in his throat, eliciting an answering growl from the beast.

Heart pounding, Lyssa pushed down the door lock. A wolf. Alex. She moaned. Alex. A wolf.

The huge beast glided forward, stopping when it was so close its nose pressed against her window. The eyes—Lyssa gasped, her heart pounding, her mouth dry. Shining bright with intelligence were Alex's amber-colored eyes.

"Oh crap," she muttered, still clutching her terrified—and furious—cat. "I'm hallucinating now. I must be."

Alex had vanished and the wolf had appeared, all at once. Further proof that she'd lost her mind. Shaking, she eyed the ignition. Alex hadn't left the key.

Sam growled again. "I know, Sam. No way are we really seeing this. We've got to get out of here."

As though he'd heard her, the giant wolf made a sound. A cross between a bark and a growl. While she tried to decide what to do, the animal stepped back, cocking his massive head and intently watching her.

Then, exactly as it had before, the wolf's shape began to waver. Sparks formed, flared and winked out of existence. The air shimmered. Lyssa stared, swallowing hard, as the wolf vanished.

Buck naked, his shoulders back, head held high, Alex stood in its place. He was the wolf. The wolf was him.

Lyssa screamed. This couldn't be happening—what she'd just seen couldn't possibly be real. The strain of the past few months had finally caused her to snap—her mind was gone. Crazy, nuts, loco.

Rubbing her eyes, she looked again.

Expression inscrutable, Alex stared at her with the wolf's eyes.

Insanity seemed the best option.

Either that or things had gotten dramatically worse. She might be married to the Bone Man.

Chapter 5

Blood pumping, heart pounding, Alex watched as Lyssa's expression went from one of disbelief to stunned shock to horror. When she screamed, he winced. With the aftereffects of *change* thrumming savagely in his veins, he turned away to compose himself.

Breathing slow and steady, he gathered up his clothing and got dressed. The spring breeze ruffled his hair, chilling his skin. With his heightened senses, he could smell grass and the heady scent of pollen—normal for April. If he tried, he could even smell the light fragrance of Lyssa's floral perfume. But the perfume could not blot out the overwhelming scent of her absolute, sheer terror. He tasted it like blood on his tongue.

She thought him a monster.

Pushing away despair, Alex pulled his shirt over his head. Hounds help him, he felt like a caged beast. He couldn't bring himself to look at her. Not yet. He didn't know how he would calm her or, worse, what he would do if he saw revulsion on her pretty face. Most humans couldn't deal with a reality in which shifters existed, thus the tales of the legendary werewolf in all its evil, and untrue, glory.

If he could have had one wish, just one, Alex would have wished Lyssa would somehow understand. Or, failing that, at least empathize. He was tired of pretending to be something he was not. Tired of lies.

But he didn't believe in fairy tales. If she accepted him, she would do so because she had to. Nothing more, nothing less. Her life depended on it.

Finally clothed, he steeled himself and raised his head to look at her. From inside the car, he could read the stark terror in her eyes as she alternated between watching him and searching for a weapon.

He moved closer, moving slowly. When he reached her side of the car, he stopped. "Lyssa, I told you I'd need to explain."

She shook her head and mouthed some words.

"I can't hear you." Moving closer he topped the window. "Roll it down."

Again she shook her head.

"Just a crack. So we can hear each other."

She hesitated, then leaned over and turned the handle just a little.

Impassive, she stared at him, her eyes huge. Had she located something to use for a weapon? He had no way to tell. The only visible sign of her agitation was the compulsive way she stroked her angry cat. Over and over her small hand went from head to tail. Sam looked like he'd take off like a shot at the first opportunity. Alex couldn't blame him.

"Don't come any closer." She gave the order in a wavering voice that didn't sound like her own. "You're him, aren't you? The Bone Man."

Recoiling, at first he could not speak. Hounds help him, she thought *he*—the thought was so awful he couldn't finish it. "No." His denial rang out, the one word not enough and yet too much. "You know better."

Sitting up straight, the accusation in her gaze never wavered. "Do I? It all makes sense now. There's no large dog, is there? A wolf ripped those women apart. *You* tore them up. You. A werewolf." A faint edge of hysteria rang in her voice.

He leaned close to make sure she could hear him. Pretended not to notice how she recoiled.

"Listen to me. This is why I decided to let you see the truth about me. You're right, the Bone Man most likely *is* a shifter and can change into a wolf, like me. I wanted you to know what we're up against, you and I. I'm not him."

She still looked doubtful, though resolute. In her hand she clutched his screwdriver, the old Phillips head he'd thrown in the glove box.

"Prove it," she said.

"How? How can I prove this to you?" He ran a hand through his hair. What could he do? How could he make her believe him? Then he knew. The connection between them. The tenuous link that had permitted him to know when she'd been attacked. Thin, true, but he'd have to rely on that. He really didn't have much else to go on.

"Think about it, Lyssa. You'd *know* if I were committing such horrible acts. Just like I knew when he attacked you." He pressed on. "*He*. Not I. Hell, I wasn't even in town the night you were assaulted."

Still wearing the shell-shocked expression of a bombing victim, she bared her teeth, a reflection of re-membered horror in her eyes. She made a sound, half-way between a laugh and a cry, sending a chill along his spine.

One hand went to her throat. "I don't know that. You could have been. Waiting, watching. You were there when Claire was killed. And then you showed up here hours after my attack."

Cursing, he pushed away the sharp stab of pain at her words. "You know me. How could you think such a thing?"

Her eyes burned. "I wonder how many other places you conveniently have been right around the time a girl was murdered."

She honestly thought he *was the killer.*

"Jeez." He ran a hand through his hair. The effects of the change continued to thrum through his veins, heady, savage. Not the aspect he needed to project now, to calm her. He struggled to gain control, to become the impassive man who had at least a prayer of making Lyssa trust him again.

"Lyssa, it wasn't me. If I wanted to kill you, to harm you, I've had plenty of opportunities, haven't I?" He spread his arms wide, palms extended. "Don't you think I would have done it long before now?"

"I—" Doubt flashed across her face. "I don't know. You don't *seem* like a serial killer, but then I've heard Jeffrey Dahmer was like the boy next door."

"You're comparing me to Jeffrey Dahmer?"

"You know what I mean."

"You know I'm not the killer."

Though she hesitated, finally she gave a small nod. Relief flooded through him. Progress, though slight.

Inhaling, he focused blindly on a point past the car, the leafy forest a mocking blur. All he could see was the horror in Lyssa's eyes.

Breath in. Out. In. Again the soft scent of the season tickled his nose. Spring. He listened, slowing his heartbeat and his breathing to normal levels. Gradually he became aware of the world again. In the forest around them, birds chirped and sang. Squirrels—prey for his wolf-self—scampered unafraid on gnarled tree branches. The earth was green in this final bloom before summer. New life abounded.

For a fleeting moment, Alex longed to change again and run in the woods, unfettered and unafraid.

Instead, fully human, he concentrated on the task at hand. "Lyssa—"

"It's locked." She threw the words out defiantly.

Locked. No point in reminding her that he had the key in his pants pocket. Not now, not yet. He wanted her to let him in, of her own volition.

She stared at him, brandishing the screwdriver. Finally, she looked away. "What did you mean when you said I'd know if you were the killer?"

He kept his gaze locked on hers. "You'd know. I told you, we're tied together, somehow, you and I. I *felt* it when you were attacked, felt his hands around your throat. And you, you sometimes know what I'm thinking. I realize you don't believe in anything beyond the ordinary, but—"

Again she shook her head, sending her blond hair flying. "And this wolf thing. I don't believe that either. What I saw wasn't possible. How did you do it?"

"I'm a shifter. I carry the genetic ability to change into a wolf."

"No. I don't buy it. It's a trick. Explain how you did it."

"It wasn't a trick. No smoke and mirrors. I changed into my wolf-self."

"No. What I saw couldn't have happened. No way. No how."

"It did. I changed into a wolf." He shifted his weight from one foot to the other, still fighting an internal battle with the need to change again. He hadn't stayed long enough in his wolf persona.

"I can't believe that."

"Believe it. Then deal with it. Despite what you choose to believe, there are things in this world not so easily explained."

Her mouth twitched. "Oh yeah? Like life after death?"

"Maybe."

"We live once and when we die, that's it. Over."

He knew she was thinking of her sister and their pact, not shifters, but he had no rebuttal. His people had debated whether or not shifters had souls for centuries.

"You're not a werewolf."

Wincing slightly at the term, he just looked at her. "Please. Open the door and let me in."

"You have the key. Why don't you use it?"

"Because I want you to trust me."

"Trust you? You must be joking." Her determined expression told him she still wasn't entirely certain about his non-killer status. "I don't want to end up dead like the others."

Only years of undercover work enabled him to keep his face expressionless. Hard to do when it feels like a steel trap closing over your chest.

"Do you really believe it was me?" At her mutinous expression, he pressed. "Honestly, take a look deep inside your heart and tell me you truly think I'm the Bone Man."

He watched her, waiting for her to back down.

She stared back, her mouth set, not giving an inch. Finally, she blinked. Then she reached over and unlocked the car.

Thank God. Crossing around to his side, he slid in, closing the door behind him.

A sharp intake of breath was her only response. Alex noted she had her back pressed up against her door, as far away from him as she could get and still remain inside the car.

Sam m-rowled.

"Now I know why Sam doesn't like you." She held her pet away from him. "And why you hate cats."

He sighed. "I'm not the Bone Man, Lyssa."

"Fine. Maybe you aren't. But what are you, exactly? What was that?" Spoken without inflection, she turned in her seat, the leather squeaking, to face Alex fully. The color blooming in her cheeks was the only visible sign of her agitation. "What the hell did I just see?"

"Like I said, I'm a shifter." Matching her tone, he gave her what he hoped was a reassuring smile. "I really can change shape from a man to a wolf."

"Okaaay. Now you're either trying to tell me I have gone crazy, or you've lost your own mind." Still petting her cat, she must have kneaded his fur too hard one time too many. Sam hissed, arching his back and batting at her.

"Sorry," she muttered. Though she stopped her overzealous petting, she kept a firm grip on the furious cat's collar. "Maybe both of us are nuts."

"No. I showed you something few humans ever see. I'm a shape-shifter. A wolf."

"A wolf."

"Yes."

"Like Michael J. Fox in that movie."

This made him smile. "Not nearly as horrific. Now are you going to drop the screwdriver?"

Lyssa lifted her hand, staring at her impromptu weapon as though she'd forgotten she still held it. Muttering to herself, she opened her fist and let the Phillips head fall to the floor. This done, she studied Alex. "A wolf. You."

No condemnation. Just a tentative attempt at understanding. At her tone, hope bloomed in his chest. Ruthlessly, he quashed it, pushing words past the tightness in his throat. "Yep. Me. I'm a wolf."

She blinked. "I—how could such a thing even be possible?"

"Possible? It's genetics, maybe a mutation. No one really knows how or when it happened, but my kind has been around for centuries."

"Your kind? There are others like you?" She didn't sound horrified now, only curious and disbelieving. Still. But anything was an improvement over her thinking he might be the Bone Man.

He smiled. "Many others. We coexist with humans, unnoticed."

"Is that where you're taking me? To the hiding place of these others?"

Her intuitive leap amazed him. "See what I mean? We have a connection. Yes, I am taking you to my

Pack—what you'd call my family. But it's not a hiding place. We don't hide ourselves, just what we can become. Most of us live normal lives."

"Most of you?"

He thought of the Bone Man. "Yes."

"So where does this Pack live?"

"Upstate. I'm taking you up there—to Leaning Tree, in the Adirondacks."

"Are they all," she swallowed, bravely keeping her chin up. "Werewolves?"

"Yes." He sighed. "Though most of us hate that term."

"Why? That's what you are, isn't it?"

"In a way, yes. But for us, a full moon is not necessary nor impelling. And the change is not horrific, or violent. When we become our wolf-selves, we retain all our human capacity for thought. Our senses are heightened, but the core part of us remains the same."

"That's a relief." She sighed. "So you don't, er, go insane or anything?"

He regarded her steadily. "Did I appear insane just now?"

Sam, apparently having had enough of confinement, chose that moment to make a bid for freedom. With a yowl, he fought to escape Lyssa's grip, clamping his teeth on her hand.

"Ow!" Jerking her hand away, she let go of his collar. The cat leaped forward, a blur of motion. Unfortunately for him, there was no place he could hide. So he hunkered on the top of the seat and hissed.

Alex winced as Sam's claws caught in his leather seats. Then he caught sight of Lyssa's hand. "You're bleeding."

"Yes." Raising her hand to her mouth, she gingerly sucked at her cut. "Small scratch. But it does hurt."

Alex couldn't look away.

"Don't tell me this makes you hungry." She gave a nervous laugh.

"In a different way than you mean. Sexually."

Her eyes widened. "Brutally honest, aren't you?"

He shrugged. "I've never forgotten the nights we—"

"Don't." Her face red, she reached for her still-enraged cat, making soothing sounds to each of his moaning growls. Once she had her pet settled, she resumed her calming touches and raised her gaze to Alex.

"You should have told me all this before."

"How could I? Neither of us intended our sham marriage to be real."

"Yes but—you know I hate lies."

"Would you have believed me?"

She opened her mouth, then closed it. "No."

"At the very least you would have thought I was on drugs."

"Or crazy."

"Exactly."

Sam hissed again. Lyssa murmured to him, her calm, soothing tone at odds with the stiff set of her slender shoulders.

Waiting, he forcibly kept himself from drumming his fingers on the steering wheel.

This time when she looked at him, he felt the force of her green gaze like a blow to his abdomen.

"Okay, so this is it then?"

"It?" Cocking his head, he waited for her to continue.

"No more surprises?"

Thinking of his suspicions about the Bone Man, he deliberated how much to tell her.

"Alex," she warned. "No more secrets."

Either his thoughts must have shown in his face or she was becoming as adept at reading him as he was her.

What the hell.

"The Bone Man—"

Resigned horror settled on her face. "I knew it! You're about to tell me you know him. You already said he's a werewolf, one of you." Horror dawned on her expressive face. "He's not some relative of yours, is he?"

"I know the only immediate blood relative I have left is my sister. I'm certain she's not the Bone Man."

"But he—the Bone Man—could be a distant cousin."

"No. I don't think so."

"But you don't know for sure."

"If I knew who the Bone Man was, we wouldn't have a problem would we?"

"We'd still have to catch him."

"I don't know him." He watched her closely. "But yes, I think he's a shifter also."

"Those poor women."

Reaching for the glove box, so he could show her his notes, Alex brushed his hand across her knee. With a sharp hiss of breath, she recoiled.

"What?" He narrowed his eyes, unwilling to let her know how much her reaction—involuntary or not—bothered him.

"Nothing."

He opened the glove box, removing the small pad of paper he kept there. Instead of discussing his theories with her, he handed her his notes and started the car.

Without another word, she began reading, keeping one hand free to contain her cat.

He glanced at the feline. Sam glared back.

"The feeling is mutual."

Lyssa raised her head. "What?"

"Just having a little conversation with your pet." He smiled. "He doesn't like me any more than I like him."

"Well for God's sake, of course not. You're a wolf, he's a cat."

Alex liked the way she said the words, with casual acceptance. Like she'd already gotten comfortable with the idea of his changing. But, because of her overreaction to his slightest movement, he knew better.

He'd give her time. As for her cat, he had his doubts the animal would ever be able to deal with him, human or otherwise.

Shifting the car into first, they pulled out, gravel spinning as Alex accelerated.

Lyssa continued to read. When she'd finished, she neatly folded the paper and placed it back inside the glove box. "Okay, so your notes make some good points. But I have to tell you, I still don't know what to think about you, him or—" she waved a hand "—this entire changing into a wolf thing."

Mrrow. Sam let it be known exactly what *he* thought.

"I'm sorry." Alex sighed.

She lifted her chin. "I really think it would be best if you turned the car around and took me back home."

"No."

"Really. I insist."

He kept his fingers wrapped around the steering wheel. "Why the sudden change of heart?"

"Do you seriously need to ask?"

"No. But I want to hear you say it."

"Fine. I don't trust you anymore. I'm not comfortable at all."

Tightening his fingers on the wheel, he kept his gaze fixed on the road. "Because of what I am?"

"I just want to go home."

"Because of what I am?"

"Maybe. Look, why'd you have to show me, tell me? I'd rather not know."

He spoke so softly his voice was almost a whisper. "Would you now? Really, would you?"

She didn't waver. "Yes."

"Even though not knowing would risk your life?"

"My life is already at risk. This guy broke into my house, for Pete's sake."

"But if you won't acknowledge the truth about what he is, you place yourself in even more danger."

"You don't know that."

"Common sense."

She exhaled. "Come on now, just because he's a werewolf doesn't mean this guy has other supernatural powers."

"No, but he's cunning and strong and crazy."

She stared at him. "There's more, isn't there? There's something you're not telling me."

"There's that connection between us again." Dryly.

"What else? What else is there about this guy that you know and haven't shared?"

Now he clenched his teeth. "What the hell. You might as well know it all."

"Damn straight. Especially since it's me he's after."

"There's a legend."

"Isn't there always?" At his glare she rolled her eyes. "A joke, Alex. Trying to lighten the tension."

He couldn't resist. "You made the tension."

She snorted. "I'm not the one who changed into a wolf."

He chose to ignore her last comment. "About the legend. I think this Bone Man believes he's reliving an old tale among my people." Quickly, he filled her in.

When he finished, she frowned. "I don't get it. What does any of this have to do with me?"

"Don't you understand? The Bone Man—or King Nebeshed—is searching for his human consort, the Queen of Light. He has to kill her and then try to bring her back to life. I think that's what he did with Claire. And most likely, tried with the others. You're the only one he didn't kill. That's why he's fixating on you."

"Great."

"I don't believe he'll use half measures this time. Until you're dead, he won't know whether you are his queen or not. He won't rest until he's killed you."

"An immortal queen? First it's werewolves, now you're telling me there are immortal beings?"

"It's a legend. That's all."

"Why not?" She threw up a hand. "Compared to everything else, the more plausible it seems. Hey, my entire life has now become totally weird." She stared him down. "You, my pretend-husband, are actually a werewolf. The Bone Man might be as well. What's next—vampires? Zombies? Ghosts? Sure, what the hell. Why not an immortal queen?"

Chapter 6

Lyssa felt like she'd entered some sort of alternate reality, like the old *Twilight Zone* television show. Surreal.

But this was real life. She rubbed her eyes. *Her* life. Not a dream, not a horrid nightmare. Real. Alex could change shape. She'd actually witnessed him becoming a wolf. Boring, normal, call-at-ten-on-a-Saturday-night-because-she's-sure-to-be-there Lyssa, who'd thought her life had become strange when she'd pretended to join a biker gang in a futile attempt to rescue her sister. Now she was trapped in a two-seater car in the middle of nowhere with a freakin' werewolf.

Yep, that summed it up nicely. But wait, it got even worse. They were on their way to a remote mountain town that happened to be chock full of even *more* werewolves.

She'd laugh out loud, but feared if she did that might

prove she'd crossed the fine line that separated sanity and madness. Hell, for all she knew, she'd crossed that boundary awhile back, when she'd started seeing men change into wolves.

A demented killer. A werewolf. No, more than one. An entire community of them.

"You're not immortal or anything, are you?"

His mouth twitched. "No, of course not. We grow old and die, just like you. We heal faster—something to do with our genetic makeup. Most of us can heal a non-fatal wound within hours."

Lyssa shot him her best glare, the one that had always caused Claire to give in. No reaction. She noticed his hands, his beautiful long-fingered hands, relaxed upon the steering wheel. No white-knuckled grip for him.

"So you can die. Then how, exactly, does one kill a werewolf?"

With a sideways glance at her, he smiled. "There are two ways. A silver bullet or with fire. That's one of the few things the books and movies got right."

A silver bullet. Fire. She, who had always abhorred violence, now contemplated the best way to take out another living being.

Kill or be killed. She clenched her fists, wondering where the savage thought came from. A second later, she knew.

"Law of the jungle." Alex sounded reasonable, though his voice was edged with anger. "When dealing with someone like this, laws and rules don't apply. It's you or him."

"I don't want any part of this."

"Whether you like it or not, you *are* part of it. But we're going to get him. I promise."

"I wish I shared your confidence. I just want my life back."

"I know." His deep voice enveloped her, touching along her raw nerve passages, soothing her.

More weirdness she didn't need.

"How did you do that?" She squinted at him. "Is it some werewolf power or something?"

To his credit, he didn't pretend not to know what she meant. "No, that has nothing to do with me being a shifter. That's between you and me—special. Different. I told you, we have a connection."

A connection. Some sort of mystical tie. Another woo-woo type of thing he wanted her to believe in.

Still, she couldn't deny some of what he said. When she'd met him in the biker gang Hades Claws, she'd felt an immediate sense of what she and Claire in their younger days had wistfully called a recognizing of souls. He'd felt it too, for when Hades Claws had wanted to initiate her by passing her around among them, he'd stepped in and claimed a prior relationship. He'd even gone so far as to marry her as the doubting biker leader Nemo had demanded, sharing a room and a bed and behaving like a perfect gentleman despite the simmering sexual attraction between them. Until she'd made the first move...

If he had been anyone else, she would have run from the car, screaming like a banshee.

But this was Alex... Alex. He'd saved her once and asked for nothing in return. The nights they'd spent entwined in each others arms haunted her, even though Alex had left again. Even now.

Now something much worse than a bunch of horny bikers was after her.

The Bone Man. She shuddered. Hard to believe she was the target of a crazed serial killer. Once again, Alex had stepped in to defend her. Why? Duty only?

"We're still married," Alex said.

Had she spoken aloud?

"I could tell what you were thinking. You're my wife."

She snorted. "Great sex does not a marriage make."

His eyes darkened at the mention of sex. "Lovemaking like we shared is unique."

"Maybe it is." She closed her eyes, fighting exhaustion as her rage left her. Through her lashes, she studied him, mentally listing his good qualities. Reliable. Strong. Firm. That he was exceptionally handsome she'd unconsciously viewed as a plus, until she'd seen him change into a wolf.

He'd said he had only a sister. She hadn't even known he *had* a sister.

"What happened to your parents?"

He blinked. "My mother died when Brenna and I were seventeen. We never knew our father."

"Brenna? Your sister?"

"My twin." He momentarily let got of the wheel in order to make an open-handed gesture. "I grew up here in upstate New York, went to college, got a degree—"

"In what?"

"Accounting."

She stared at him in disbelief. "But you work for the DEA."

"So? They don't care what degree you have, as long as you have one." He smiled. "What else would you like to know about me? Let's see. After I graduated, I traveled. Seattle, Vancouver, Boise, Bismark, Phillie, Boston. Never been married, no kids. There. Now you know everything."

"Everything?"

"Pretty much."

"How do you feel, since you don't have any secrets from me now?"

His smile broadened, though his eyes remained serious. "I trust you, Lyssa. Otherwise I'd never have shown you my changing."

Changing. Such a simple word. Yet forever now she would see the sparkles of light, the soft glow as his limbs became elongated, as his muscular, human form became that of a giant, silver wolf.

A *beautiful* giant wolf. She had to give him that. As he was in human form, so he was as an animal. Superb. And to be totally honest, after the initial shock, she'd never felt the slightest bit threatened or in danger. Other than trying to adjust to the fact that such things truly existed, she had no reason to be afraid.

This was Alex. Alex Lupe, undercover DEA, always-do-the-right-thing, protect-the-underdog Alex. No matter what else he might be, she needed to remember that.

She let her tight shoulders sag, trying to force the remaining tension from her. "No more lies, Alex."

"Agreed. No more lies between us." He didn't even hesitate. "Do you have any more questions?"

"Not now." Most likely she would have questions, after she'd had time to think. Gazing out the window, she watched as mile after mile of shadowy forest went past. The farther north they traveled, the less inhabited the landscape. The wilds of northern New York. The sparsely populated Adirondack Mountains were still primitive in many ways. She shook her head, chastising herself. Where else would she expect werewolves to live? Certainly not in the middle of New York City.

But they apparently did fine in a place called Leaning Tree. She'd never heard of Leaning Tree, New York. But then she'd never believed in werewolves either.

She tried to focus on her rapidly shrinking comfort zone. Where before the throaty growl of Alex's car had soothed, now the sound seemed primal and threatening.

Werewolves. If *they* existed, and she'd seen Alex change with her own eyes, then what else might be real? What other shadowy creatures walked in the night?

"One thing at a time," she muttered.

"What did you say?" One corner of his well-shaped mouth lifted with amusement. No doubt he'd heard her, especially if he had the superior hearing of a wolf.

Damn! She shook her head. From the frying pan into the fire.

"It's not quite that bad," he said, again as though he'd read her mind. "My kind has been around for thousands of years."

For some reason, the pride in his voice surprised her. "You talk as though your heritage makes you proud."

"I'm not ashamed of what I am. My lineage is an old and honorable one."

Honorable. Werewolf. The two seemed an oxymoron.

She peered at him. "How are you going to explain me to them, these people you're taking me to see?"

"Explain you? What do you mean?"

"Do you habitually bring women to meet them?"

He shook his head no.

Despite everything, relief flooded her. Talk about confusing.

"How well do you know them?"

"What do you mean?"

"This "pack", these people. You said you had no family except your sister."

His brow cleared. "This is the town where Brenna and I grew up. Even though we have no other blood relations, the townspeople sort of adopted us."

"The village raising the kid thing?"

"Sort of."

"Surely you didn't tell them about your pretend marriage?"

He shot her a look. "Of course not."

She heard what he didn't say as clearly as if he'd spoken the words out loud. *Not yet. But I intend to.*

"How will you introduce me?"

"As my wife." As if that said it all. The certainty with which he spoke resonated in the confined car interior.

"I thought we agreed no more lies?"

"It's not a lie, not technically. We *are* married." He shifted in his seat, the leather creaking. "Do you see another choice? I can't relay the news that I'm bringing you home to protect you from a crazed serial killer."

"Why not?"

"Think about it. The entire town might erupt in mass panic. I have to speak to the council first, find out what they want me to do."

"Fine." She sighed. "Why do you have to tell them anything at all? Why lie? If you say nothing, they'll just assume I'm your friend or something."

"They know me well enough to realize I wouldn't bring just any woman home. No, you are my wife." Certainty rang in his voice. "One thing I have learned from years undercover is that it's better to stick to one falsehood if you want people to believe you're telling the truth. We've already told Trask and the locals that we're married. I don't want to change stories midstream."

"Thanks for the crash course in lying. You forget, I used to live with the queen of falsehoods." She knew she sounded bitter, but there was no help for it. "Why can't we tell them the truth?"

"Please." He met her gaze, his expression implacable. "Trust me on this. If it makes things easier, pretend we're undercover."

Pretend. More proof that Alex had difficulty distinguishing between what was true and what wasn't. Yet another battle she couldn't hope to win. "Fine, but how are you going to explain keeping your marriage a secret?"

He shrugged. "I hadn't thought about it. They know I'm a DEA agent."

"What does that have to do with anything?"

"I keep lots of secrets."

She sat up as a thought occurred to her. "Is there some law among your people about marrying a non-wolf-person?"

"A non-shifter?" With a quick smile, he shook his head. "No. My own sister married a human. He learned to keep one eye closed."

"One eye closed?" she repeated. "As in, look the other way?"

He nodded. "Sometimes that's best when humans deal with us."

Human. Nonhuman. Like an alien from another planet. Oh no, she wouldn't go there. Taking a deep breath, she stared out the window, thinking. Something about the legend nagged at her....

"Hey, there's a flaw with your immortal queen theory."

He glanced at her. "What?"

"If this King Nebeshed and his queen were truly immortal, they'd still be around, wouldn't they?"

He glanced at her, his gaze dark. "My ancestors killed her the same way she was brought to life. She was created with a rib bone. After a fierce battle, they removed that which created her. Once the rib bone had been destroyed, they set her on fire and her unnatural life was finished as well."

His words brought to mind bloody images of teeth and claws.

"What about him?"

"King Nebeshed was killed by fire also. When he died, his ashes were placed in an ancient clay vessel, carefully constructed, which was weighted and thrown into the ocean. It sank to the bottom of the sea, where it remains until this day."

"Do you think the Bone Man found it? Is that why he believes he's Nebeshed?"

"I doubt it. If such a thing even existed, this would have been centuries ago. No one even knows what sea the legend references."

"Oh." Lyssa decided to concentrate on the scenery rather than obtaining answers she didn't want to hear.

The more the road twisted and curved, the higher they climbed. The lush forests of the Hudson Valley thinned. The trees seemed both more fragile and more sturdy at the same time, appealing to Lyssa in ways she could not explain.

"We're almost there."

"This looks familiar," she murmured. "I don't know why."

"You've never gone upstate?"

"I never had a reason. How long has it been since you were here?"

"Recently. I was here the night you were attacked, watching baseball with Carson, my sister's husband."

Her *human* husband.

"He used to be your partner? I think I met him once. Wasn't he the guy Hades Claws hated? The one whose family got murdered?"

"Yes. He took a job with the Leaning Tree police force once he and Brenna got married."

Lyssa decided to make a point of finding this Carson and talking to him. It'd be interesting to see what he thought of all this shape-shifter stuff. A normal man's take on the life she now found herself reluctantly immersed in.

Except he wasn't being stalked by some serial killer who also happened to be a werewolf.

Lyssa sat up straight. "If the Bone Man's one of you, how do you know he won't be here, too? What if taking me to Leaning Tree is like bringing a sacrificial virgin to the volcano?"

He grinned. "You're no virgin."

"You know what I mean." Despite that, she felt her cheeks color. "Have you thought about that?"

"I have. He won't be here. He has no reason to think you know about him, about the Pack. You're human and would stay in human towns. He's obsessed with you. He'll be hunting you out there. He has no reason to think you'd come here. No reason at all."

Good to know. She wished she could be as certain. "He doesn't know you're a…a shifter?"

"He might. We tend to recognize each other. But I

doubt if he even saw me, he paid any attention. Like I said, my people are everywhere. It wouldn't be unusual to see another shifter, even in a motorcycle gang."

"Doubt." She pounced on the word. "Not a hundred-percent certain. How can you be sure he won't look here?"

"Don't worry about it. No one knows where we've gone."

Still she persisted. "What if he's put a tracer on your car? It's possible."

"Yes, but unlikely. I think he's too busy trying to stay hidden. The FBI, the police, they're all hunting this guy. He's got to feel the noose tightening."

"But won't Trask eventually want to know where we've gone? Then, once you tell him, what if there's a leak? You could be endangering your family."

"Trask knows you're with me. But if it will make you feel better, I'll make a quick call on my cell phone. I'll tell him we went to a safe house somewhere else, like Rhode Island."

"More lies."

He sighed. "Sometimes they're necessary."

Despite herself, she had to concede the point. "You really think the Bone Man has access to inside information?"

"No." He flashed a smile. "*You* think that. Me, I don't know. But if just in case, this will throw him off. He seems to be focused on the Catskills. Marty, the FBI profiler, thinks he's still in Wicket Hollow. He'll look there for you first."

And others. Any other slender blonde might be fair game, if Alex's legend was the Bone Man's reason for killing.

She shivered. "I don't want anyone else to get hurt. Or killed."

"None of us do. We're gonna catch him."

"You sound sure."

"Sooner or later he'll make a mistake. When he does, I want to be there."

He sounded fierce, predatory. *Dangerous.*

She thought of the huge silver wolf, watching her with Alex's beautiful eyes. She'd best remember what he was.

"Me, too," she said, but Alex wasn't listening. He punched a number into his cell. Holding the phone to his ear, he spoke a few words in a low voice before snapping it closed.

"Did you call Trask?"

"Not yet. I let my aunt Elaine—that's what I call her, even though she's not really my aunt—know we're nearly there. We'll be staying with her. She likes to cook, so be prepared for a feast."

Lyssa nodded, though she wasn't sure she could eat. She kept picturing the other victims, smiling in the FBI photos, all tortured, all missing a rib. All dead.

And the Bone Man was still at large. Looking for her, waiting for her. When she remembered his hands around her neck, her throat closed up and she couldn't breathe. Even thinking about Alex becoming a wolf was better than that. She glanced at the screwdriver on the floor between her feet. Not much of a weapon. She wanted silver bullets and a gun. She needed to learn how to shoot.

Sam meowed, his plaintive sound. Her cat hated car rides. He'd usually hide under her back seat. Alex's sports car had no place for Sam to hide, so he now crouched inside the carryall and glared up at her. Glad of the distraction, Lyssa focused on making her pet more comfortable.

Though he pretended not to, Alex kept a close eye on Lyssa. Watching him change, she'd experienced a shock and, while she appeared to be coping with the knowledge, he still picked up on lingering panic and fear.

Hell, he couldn't blame her. Carson was the only human Alex knew whose first reaction wasn't instinctive terror. Maybe that was because in his job as an undercover DEA agent, Carson had seen things that would drive most other people mad.

Tension crackled in the air. He felt it, around them, between them, roiling and sizzling. Sexual energy. Briefly, Alex thought of the change, and the way his body felt electrified as he became a wolf. Similar to sex, the change from human to wolf and back again was a prelude to actual intercourse among many shifters.

Great sex does not a marriage make. Lyssa's words haunted him. They'd been good together—no, they'd been on fire together. The brief kiss they'd shared told him they hadn't lost that. He eyed Lyssa, her beauty as always tightening his throat. Would she let him touch her now, knowing what he was? Or would she pull away in horror?

Suddenly, knowing the answer became more important than breathing.

As though subliminally picking up on his thoughts, Lyssa stared at him, wide-eyed, and parted her lips.

Hell hounds! His body surged in response. With a swift twist of his wrist on the wheel, he pulled over to the grassy shoulder. Leaving the engine running, he pushed the gearshift into park. Heart pounding, blood pumping, he unbuckled his seat belt and turned toward her.

"Wha…?" Her nipples pushed against her T-shirt, betraying her own arousal.

Man…or beast? How would she see him now?

He leaned in close, intent on her mouth.

Ahh. As he'd thought—current flowed between them.

"Alex." She met him halfway. Covered his lips with hers and kissed him. Hard.

Man.

"Damn." Alex felt her hand on him. Helpless against the force of his arousal, he surged against her. She'd surprised him.

He heard a groan, dimly recognizing the sound of his own voice. She rocked against him, answering his cry with one of her own. His body, already hyperaware, thickened. His blood, change-charged, rushed through his veins. He was barely able to hold on to his shredded self-control.

Lyssa clawed at him, whimpering low in her throat. Eyes dark with passion, she climbed over the gearshift to settle in his lap, her back pressed to the wheel, the heat of her center over his raging arousal.

Everything sharpened. *His mate.* The thought came with startling clarity.

She cried out, her mouth on his. He tasted her, touched her, cupped her breasts, and pulled her shirt over her head. She spilled from her bra into his hands, and he bent his lips to suckle her. Rolling her nipple between his teeth and tongue, he felt savage, about to explode. Her scent surrounded him, the soft musk of her desire mingling with her perfume.

Lifting herself off him, she moved back into her seat. One tug of his zipper, and she freed him. Stroked him, brought him nearly to the moment of release so quickly he gasped and nearly bit her tongue.

"Don't," he managed to say. That one word, hoarsely uttered, merely made her hesitate. When she lowered her mouth and closed her lips over him, heat replaced rational thought. He fumbled for her jeans, for the zipper, wanting to touch her, to place his finger inside her warmth.

At that moment, apparently tired of being squished, Sam let out a yowl of warning and slashed his claws at Alex's arm.

Alex broke away. Heart pounding, his breathing came harsh and fast. Staring at him with wide eyes, Lyssa looked as stunned as he felt. In the confined space, her chest rose and fell, her breathing as agitated as his.

Agitated? Hell, aroused.

Blood welled from the scratch on his arm. The damn cat crouched as though it wanted to attack again. Alex swore Sam licked his lips.

"What the hell?" Lyssa glanced at her pet, then back at him. Both she and her cat watched him with identical, wary expressions. She looked down at his arousal. "You're…"

Very conscious that she still held him in her hand, he closed his fingers over hers, gently prying her loose and tucking himself back into his jeans.

With her head held high and her cheeks blazing scarlet, she climbed back into her own seat, pulling up her bra over her breasts and grabbing her shirt off the floor. Only when she'd rearranged her clothing to her satisfaction did she look at him again.

"What just happened here?"

He thought of several different responses, discarding them instantly. She needed raw honesty now. "I don't know."

"But you're a…earlier I saw you change into a wolf."

"Does that make a difference?" He kept his voice casual, unwilling to let her know how much her answer mattered.

"Apparently not." Her expression hardened. "We've always been great together Alex, but I felt like an animal myself, totally out of control. We're in your car, for Pete's sake! Almost at your aunt's house."

Her words pleased him. "You've accepted what I am."

"Maybe. Maybe not. I haven't had enough time to process it all. Your timing sucks, Alex. What were you thinking?" She gestured at the windows, at the still deserted road.

"I didn't intend for it to go so far. After I changed…" he hesitated. "I didn't stay long enough as a wolf."

"So you were scratching an itch? Is that what you're saying?"

"No." At a loss for words, he willed the connection between them to kick in and make her understand.

Apparently, it didn't. Anger flared in her eyes. "Don't tell me that was your idea of seduction?"

"Seduction?" The thought had never occurred to him. At least, not in context with her. Lyssa was…Lyssa. Close. Warm. Heat to his flame.

"Yeah, seduction." Shaking her head, she looked away. "Courtship. You know, what people do when they don't have an insane serial killer after them."

Frustrated, he started to reach for her, but caught

himself in time. "Lyssa, of course I've been wanting to make love to you." He hesitated, then decided. If she wanted the truth, he'd give it to her. "Tell me you haven't thought about it, how good it would feel with me buried inside you. Tell me you haven't remembered how you came apart every time we made love."

Though her pupils darkened, she frowned. "I have thought about it, about us. But we've already agreed to concentrate on the Bone Man, not the one thing we managed to get right in our pretend marriage. We need to focus on that. Remember?"

Focus. He felt the word like a surprise right hook to the jaw. That word had been his mantra, the way he'd kept from falling apart when Carson's family had been murdered and he'd arrived too late to stop the killing.

Lyssa was right. They had no time for playing around. Not now. Not until the Bone Man was either dead or behind bars.

Focus. Alex Lupe never lost focus. Never.

Until now.

He'd do his damnedest to make sure it didn't happen again. Clenching his teeth, he shifted from park to drive. Lyssa's life—and his own as well—could very well depend on that.

Chapter 7

"It won't happen again," he all but snarled. "You have my word."

Giving him a long, considering look, she shook her head. "Is your word any good?"

"Ouch." He winced. "I suppose I deserved that. But Lyssa, when I met you, I was undercover. Pretending to be something I'm not came with my job."

"And now?"

"Pretending to be—" he clenched his teeth, forcing himself to go on "—*human* is part of my life."

She swallowed. He couldn't help but notice the graceful line of her throat.

Focus.

Right. He dragged his gaze back to the road.

"Speaking of that, one other thing has occurred to me." Lyssa sounded thoughtful. "If this Bone Man really is one of you and the media finds out, what would happen to your people?"

While he'd have liked to pretend he didn't know what she meant, he knew all too well. The potential for disastrous consequences had been one of his biggest worries ever since he'd learned the Bone Man's MO.

"The Pack will have to deal with that."

She focused on his words. "Deal with it how?"

"I don't know. I need to tell the council."

"The council?"

"Our government. We—the Pack that is—have them in each state."

Though she nodded, he could see the idea that the Pack was so organized disturbed her. Her next question confirmed it.

"Exactly how many are you?"

He played it casual, lifting one shoulder in a shrug. "I'm not sure. I know there are several thousand in up-state New York, several hundred in Leaning Tree."

She gasped. "Several hundred? In one town?"

"Yeah." He let that fact sink in for a moment before continuing. "We live all over the country."

"Only in the U.S.A.?"

"No. Europe. Asia. Africa, too."

"Basically, you're everywhere."

He nodded. "And have been for centuries."

"How is it no one has discovered any of this? Surely with that many…"

"Oh, there are those who think they know the truth. They write books, tell stories. Most rational people dismiss them as crackpots."

Her expression dazed, she dipped her chin. "Like the alien abductions."

Though he chuckled, he found it a bit rankling that she'd compared him to that. "I don't know about those."

"Hey, if werewolves are real…"

He laughed. She smiled in return, despite everything.

His cell phone rang. Unclipping it from his belt, he answered.

"Where the hell are you?" It was Trask, sounding uncharacteristically panicked. "Lyssa's gone. No one knows where she went, or how."

"She's with me."

A string of virulent curses followed. Alex held the phone away from his ear until Trask had finished.

"Calm down. I'm taking her to a safe house."

"On whose authority?" The other man barked.

"My own. She's my wife, dammit."

"Where are you taking her?"

"Rhode Island." The lie came easy, like always. In the course of his undercover career, Alex had become used to duplicity. Too used to it, he sometimes thought. Now he was tired. He glanced at his watch. "We've been gone well over an hour. It took your people too damn long to realize she was gone."

Silence for a moment, while the other man digested his words. Finally, Trask sighed. "I know. Believe me when I tell you my men got their asses chewed."

Alex couldn't help but grin. The two Trask had assigned to guard duty had been young, first year in the field, he'd bet.

"It, uh—" Trask cleared his throat "—gets even worse."

"Worse? What the hell happened?"

"Lyssa's house is, ah, gone. Torched. That's when we realized she was missing."

"What?" Alex glanced at Lyssa. Still watching him,

intent, she stiffened, as though she somehow knew. "What the hell?"

"Your wife's house. He torched it. Went up in flames. Burned to the ground."

Damn. "When?"

"Maybe an hour ago. Must've been right after you left. The bastard slipped in, knocked out the two locals—let his damn dog attack one. Nearly ripped out his throat."

Alex cursed. Maybe that's why no one caught them leaving.

"There's more. While we were trying to put that fire out, the SOB torched her shop. All her plants burned. There's nothing left. The fire department is still spraying the embers. The arson investigator is going over it now."

Fire. One of their kind's most feared enemies. Yet the Bone Man had used it indiscriminately, apparently without fear.

Keeping one hand on the steering wheel, Alex fought the urge to rub the back of his neck. "How the hell did that happen? Don't tell me nobody saw him."

A long silence from Trask. Finally he answered, his voice sounding even more weary. "You got out without anyone noticing. There was a full retinue around the place. No one saw him. But we were close. So close I can taste it—my men actually saw his dog. Thing's as big as a wolf. Might be a wolf hybrid."

Alex's heart began to pound. "A wolf?"

"Yeah." Trask sighed. "Huge beast, they said. Sidling along the edge of the woods, like it was watching. I didn't see it. If I had, I would have shot the damn thing."

"It got away?"

"Yeah. Slipped into the woods before anyone thought to squeeze off a shot."

The Bone Man.

"Listen——" Alex projected command into his voice "——tell them no matter what, if they ever see the wolf again, they're to shoot to kill. Got that?"

"Got it." Trask's dry tone came across the line, laced with curiosity. "What's the deal? What do you know?"

"Just a hunch. I couldn't explain it in a million years." Not and make the other man believe him.

Trask cursed. "Look Lupe. I'm tired, I'm pissed, and I don't have time for this. If you know something, tell me."

"Nothing concrete. Sorry."

With a loud sigh, Trask let it go.

"Anything else?"

"Yeah. One more bit of bad news. I think your wife's cat might have perished in the fire. The firefighters looked, but they found no sign of it. You'll have to break the news to her. Not only did she lose her home, and her business, but she lost her pet as well."

He glanced at Lyssa, ignoring the question she mouthed at him. "The cat's fine. Lyssa took him with her."

The FBI agent whistled. "How'd you get past the guards without anyone suspecting anything?"

"It could be that we left just as the Bone Man took out the guards, or when they were distracted by the wolf."

"Damn. No wonder this perp has no problem breaking in. I'm glad the cat's okay."

"A cat person, are you?"

"Maybe." Trask snorted. "I have one or two of my

own. Either way, I don't believe in letting animals—any animal—suffer needlessly. Where in Rhode Island is this safe house?"

The sudden change in subject didn't faze Alex. It was a particular tactic he'd also employed on occasion. "You don't need to know. She'll be safer that way."

Silence again. Alex could picture the other man chewing the end off a pencil. The last time the FBI and DEA had collaborated, Trask had gone through an entire package of yellow number twos.

"FBI is in charge of this operation. I'm SAC and need to know."

SAC—Special Agent in Charge. Technically, that would make Trask Alex's superior. Alex thought fast.

"The line's not secured."

Now Trask cursed. "Use a landline next time."

"Who says there'll be a next time?" Alex clicked the phone shut, flipping the power button to Off before it could ring again.

"What's happened? Was that Trask? I heard you mention a wolf." Lyssa had gone pale, as though she already knew.

"Yes." He tried to stall. "Seems the Bone Man was lurking around Wicket Hollow like I thought. They saw a large wolf."

"And?" She crossed her arms. "From what I could hear, there's more."

"Yeah, there's more. It's a good thing we got out."

In a few short words he relayed what Trask had told him. When he'd finished, he braced himself for her reaction. He expected hysterics or, at the least, tears. After all, she'd lost everything.

Despite that, she simply twisted her hands together in her lap and looked down at them. "I see."

He didn't know what to make of her reaction.

"Lyssa?" Cautiously. "Do you understand what I just said?"

"Yes." She nodded. "I have no place to live. My home is gone. All my clothing, my furniture, everything, gone. Oh, and my livelihood—my business. I have nothing left. Nothing." She spoke as though about someone else. Impersonal. Removed.

Taking her cell phone from her purse, she pushed the button to turn it on, staring at it while it registered and the signal connected.

"You leave it off?"

"Yes. Everyone always teases me about that." Her voice was still monotone, her lips tight.

"It kind of defeats the purpose."

She met his gaze, her expression unreadable. "I like to conserve the battery. Recharging it is a hassle and I always forget."

"Who are you calling?"

"I need to call Marilee. You met her—the blonde at the desk." She began punching in numbers. "Marilee runs the shop for me. I want to make sure she's all right."

He nodded, watching while she listened. Trask hadn't mentioned any other casualties.

"No answer." She cleared her throat. With a sigh, she clicked the phone closed. "Her answering machine picked up. I'll leave my cell on in case she checks her caller ID and calls me. If not, I'll try her again later."

"I'm sure she's fine. Trask would have mentioned if she weren't."

She turned to look at him. Her green eyes burned. "Damn the Bone Man." She spoke through clenched teeth. "This is one more thing to hold against him, one more reason to make him pay."

"Lyssa—"

"He'll pay for this. That, I can promise."

While part of him—the wolf part—approved of such fierceness in a potential mate, his human side was more cautious.

"Let the authorities handle it. Hell, let *me* handle it."

She smiled. If she'd been a shifter, he would have said her smile was a deadly thing. "Whatever."

"You can't go after this guy. Not alone."

"I know. You're going with me."

He shook his head. "No way. I work better alone. I'd be less effective if I have to worry about you."

"I can go after him with you, or I can go without you. Either way, I'm going. Your choice."

"Lyssa…"

"I've already told you. I refuse to sit on my butt and do nothing."

"You don't even know how to shoot a gun."

"You're going to teach me. And we'll get some silver bullets."

"Of course." Sarcasm dripped from his tone. "Any idea how? Or where?"

"No. But I'm sure you'll figure out a way." Softly, she mocked him back.

As the serpentine road wound around the base of the mountain, Alex brought himself to an inner stillness. He felt Lyssa studying him, watching him.

"You've changed again," she said.

Turning his head to regard her, he lifted a brow in question. "I haven't changed. I'm still human."

"Not that kind of change. I know you make few wasted body movements, but you've gone so still now, you could be a living, breathing statue."

"I'm alert."

"You're more than that. If I make you look at me, I think I might even find a spark of eagerness in your eyes."

"I'm always eager to go home, to see family."

"I can't win." She threw up her hands. "Now you're twisting my words."

His face went cold. Distant. "I'm good at what I do."

Undercover work. Lies. She sighed. "Tell me about your family. I feel at a disadvantage."

His response was a quick shake of the head. "Don't worry about it. You'll be fine."

When the first homes on the outskirts of town appeared, he noticed Lyssa gripping the door handle, white-knuckled. "What's wrong?"

"A town full of shape-shifters!" she said. "I don't know what to expect."

He smiled. "It's just like any other small town."

Fully restored Victorian homes, their jewel-like colors contrasting with the primitive landscape, sat proud and stately among towering pines. Every now and then she saw an occasional rustic cabin. They passed a park, complete with playground and picnic tables.

"Seriously. How do I act? Do I pretend I don't know?"

He turned up his smile a notch into a full-force grin. "They'll expect you to know since you're with me."

Great. "Does that mean they'll...*you know* in front of me?"

"Change?"

She nodded.

"Not unless they have a really good reason to. We don't usually go around changing into our wolf-selves while in human surroundings."

"Good." She sighed. "One less worry in a list that seems to grow longer by the moment."

As though sensing her tension, Sam gave a small mew and hunkered down in the bag, ears flat against his head, green eyes peering up at her.

"Then there's the cat." Alex knew his voice sounded flat.

"Promise me he won't be in any danger."

"Of course he won't. Though you'll probably have to confine him to a room."

"Definitely. Poor thing. He'll be one lone cat in a place full of wolves. Sam won't be thrilled."

One more twist of the road and they were downtown. Alex slowed the car to a crawl, motor purring.

Various shops, including a root-beer stand complete with carhops on roller skates, lined both sides of the tree-lined street. Leaning Tree High, a three-story, faded brick building built in the early 1900s, sat squat and square at the corner of Main Street and Twelfth.

"That's where I went to school."

"This place looks like something out of the fifties."

He agreed. Leaning Tree was, in his sister Brenna's words, quaint and sweet, a good place to raise children, an even better place to grow old together.

"Look!" Lyssa gasped, pointing.

In the center of the street sat a huge black wolf. Watching. Waiting.

Alex slowed the car, then stopped a full twenty feet away. Undeterred, the animal continued to stare.

"Do you know him? Or her?" Lyssa asked, her tone dry.

Though he knew she was half joking, he took her question seriously. "Maybe. Right now I have no way of knowing."

"You have no way of knowing?"

"Not without smell. If I were close enough, I could identify him by his scent."

As though listening, the wolf cocked his head. The beast's silver eyes seemed bright with intelligence.

Human intelligence. Alex wouldn't put it past one of his numerous cousins to play some sort of joke, especially if Aunt Elaine had spread the news about his return home.

"That's one big wolf." Lyssa sounded falsely bright. "I'd think you'd be able to tell who—"

"There are a lot of us here." He softened his tone. "All sizes and shapes. Black wolves are more common than you know. I don't recognize him." He eased the gas pedal down. The car inched forward. Shaking his head, the wolf loped off across a deserted baseball field and disappeared into the trees.

They both stared after it.

"You know, that might have been only a wolf."

She sighed. "Or not. It might have been one of you. Damn." She hit the dash with her fist. "I don't know if I can do this."

He tried to understand her perspective, but couldn't. "Why? Because you saw a wolf? That's pretty common, anywhere in the northern forests."

"Yeah, but how do I know that wolf," she swallowed, "won't change into a person? Or vice versa? I know you said it won't happen, but seriously—I could be standing around talking to someone and—bam—they become a wolf. That's pretty unsettling."

He shook his head, biting back a smile at the image her words provided. "We don't do that. Like I told you, most of us go into the woods to change."

"Alone?"

"Or with others. We are the Pack, after all. Does it bother you that much?" Still keeping his speed below the posted thirty-miles-per-hour limit, Alex glanced at her. She sat stiff and tense, gripping the door handle with one hand, the other clenched in her lap.

"Bother me? Actually, yes. Come on, Alex. This is the stuff of nightmares."

Though her honesty shouldn't have stung, it did.

"Surely not that bad." He kept his tone light. No way was he letting her know how much her acceptance mattered to him. "Different, yes. But being different doesn't necessarily mean bad."

She cocked her head, considering. "Let me put this in perspective for you. If I took you to a deserted field and summoned a spaceship down from the sky, then told you I was from the planet Antares or something, wouldn't you be freaked out?"

Again he found himself chuckling. "What is it with you and the alien thing? Yeah, I might think it a little odd, but you'd still be Lyssa. Alien or earthling, you yourself wouldn't have changed."

She pounced on his last word. "But you did, Alex. Change. Right in front of me."

"It's only the package."

"The package?"

"Yes." He turned right, onto a gravel road that wound into the trees. "External, not what's inside. That never changes. By the way, we're nearly there."

She jumped. Her hand went to her throat. "Great."

"You'll like Aunt Elaine. Wait and see."

"We're not staying with your sister?"

"She's a newlywed. I figured I'd give her some space."

They rounded a curve and Aunt Elaine's house came into view. Like the Victorians they'd seen as they'd driven through town, the two-story house had been fully restored. Alex's aunt had chosen to paint her home what Alex privately thought of as light orange, though Aunt Elaine insisted it was a lovely shade of peach.

He parked behind an ancient Suburban, killing the motor before he turned to face Lyssa.

"You'll be fine." He used his best reassuring, officer-of-the-law voice.

"I know that," she snapped. "I'm just not looking forward to this."

"This?"

"You know." Waving her hand in the general direction of the house, she sighed. "Meeting other were-wolves. I still haven't digested the entire idea."

"Shifters." Keeping his tone gentle, he touched her arm. She jumped. "Not werewolves. Shifters."

"What does it matter?"

"It matters to us. Believe me when I say it will matter to my aunt."

"Fine. Shifters." From the look of mistrust on her face, she might have been attending a hanging.

He got out of the car before he said something he'd regret. Going around to her side and opening the door for her, he held out his hand.

She scrambled from the low-slung car without taking it, grabbing her cat bag and holding it close. Sam let out a yowl. After murmuring a few soothing words to her pet, Lyssa hung back as she studied the house.

"It's beautiful."

"Hard to imagine a savage living here." He couldn't resist the jab.

Ignoring his comment, she stalked ahead of him to the wide front porch. Before climbing the steps, she turned to face him, keeping her bag close to her side. "You're not planning to leave me here, are you?"

"Of course not."

"Good. Because I wouldn't stay."

"Lyssa—"

"A safe house is one thing. This... I can't help but feel you've brought me to the lion's den."

"Hey." He caught her arm. She shook him off. "The Bone Man isn't here."

"You don't know that. You don't even know who he is."

About to reply, he shut his mouth as the front door swung open. Aunt Elaine, wearing one of her usual brightly colored dresses, stepped out onto the porch.

"Alex?" Her pale blue gaze swung to Lyssa. "Welcome home! And who's this?" Without waiting for his answer, she moved forward. An anklet made of tiny bells tinkled as she walked. Her assorted bracelets and bangles jangled merrily. She even wore two jeweled combs in her wavy, silver hair. As usual, Elaine glittered when she walked.

Lyssa stared. Noticing, Elaine grinned.

"A bit much, aren't I?"

"No," Lyssa stammered. "Of course not. I—"

Elaine held up her hand. "It's all right, honey. I do like my trinkets."

"Two rings on each finger." Alex grinned as he said it, knowing Elaine lived for the attention.

"Don't forget my toes," she quipped, lifting one sandaled foot. "I just love toe rings!"

"And red nail polish."

"And ankle bracelets." She smiled.

Leaning in to kiss Elaine's cheek, Alex slipped his arm around her shoulders. She smelled of lilacs, a new scent for her.

Unfortunately, it made him sneeze.

"Bless you."

Through all of this, Lyssa said not a word. Alex glanced at her, noticing the bright spots of color that stained her pale cheeks.

"Lyssa, meet Aunt Elaine." He swallowed, taking a deep breath before dropping the bombshell. "Aunt Elaine, this is Lyssa. My wife."

He'd chosen whom to tell first deliberately. Not only was Aunt Elaine the least threatening of his close acquaintances, but she loved to talk. By nightfall, everyone in Leaning Tree would know he'd acquired a wife.

At the news, Elaine squealed and punched his arm. "Wife? You secretive boy, you! I can't believe it." She swept forward, gathering Lyssa in a fierce embrace. "Welcome to the family!"

Lyssa winced. "Thank you."

For the first time since he'd become an undercover agent, Alex felt bad telling a lie. Only slightly, as he still viewed the story as necessary.

Elaine wrinkled her nose. "I smell…?"

Shifting her bag from one arm to another, Lyssa glanced at Alex. He shrugged.

"Mwrrrowl." Sam's growl came at the same moment he decided he wanted out of the bag.

"What the heck was that?" Nostrils twitching, Elaine frowned. "Feline?" She sounded delighted, making Alex squint at her.

Lyssa lifted her chin. "My cat, Samuel Adams."

"A cat?" Elaine raised her eyebrows. "You married a cat person?"

"Now Aunt Elaine, it's not as bad as it looks."

"It's certainly not." Bristling, Lyssa cradled the bag to her chest. "Sam is my baby. I won't let anyone hurt him."

"Hurt him?" Aunt Elaine huffed. "Who said anything about hurting him? I love cats, adore them. I'd have one or two of my own, but most cats won't stay with a shifter." Come on inside." Leading the way, Elaine held open the screen door for them. "Bring your baby."

Lyssa looked at Alex.

He winked. "Go ahead. You'll love the inside."

"What about you?"

"I'll be a minute. I need to call Trask. I want to find out how the wounded cops are doing and if anything else has happened."

Head held high, Lyssa stepped past him, into the house. As soon as the screen door slammed closed behind her, Alex hit Redial.

Trask answered, sounding frustrated. "You're not going to believe this."

"What's happened now?"

"The Bone Man might be on the move. Just a few minutes ago, a girl was assaulted outside a mall in Poughkeepsie. She fits the profile."

Chapter 8

Alex checked his watch. "That's more than an hour away from you. Are you sure he did it?"

"No." Trask ground his teeth, a grating sound. "We don't think so. The media is running with it, of course. And that seems to have convinced the local police."

"Any correlation?"

"Not really. The victim saw a large dog right before she was attacked, though the dog didn't bite her. Just like the dog—or wolf—my men saw near Lyssa's house. So it's possible." But Trask's tone said he didn't believe it.

"Saw—is she alive?"

"Yeah. If this was the Bone Man, then he's tried and missed a second time, now. If this was him—and I have my doubts—he's growing careless. But if that's the case, we'll get him soon."

"I agree with you. It wasn't him." Turning away, Alex walked farther down the porch. No need for Lyssa and his aunt to hear. "He wouldn't have missed. Not so late in the game. The stakes are too high."

"The only thing that even matches is the large dog."

"How long until you can convince the media?" Alex checked his watch again. "The news is coming on in ten minutes. We don't need a statewide panic."

"I've got a man working on a statement now. Should be out in time for the news."

"Any other sightings? Threats?"

"Nope." Instead of sounding happy, Trask sounded even glummer. "We can't find the SOB. The Bone Man seems to have hunkered down for now. As the hunt intensifies, he'll grow more savage, sloppy in a different way. And I agree, he wouldn't miss."

"It's got to be a copycat."

"My feelings exactly." Trask sighed. "Even the location's wrong."

Alex hadn't thought of that. But Trask was right. The Bone Man stayed near woods. So far his every attack had been in the less-populated Catskill Mountains, not in crowded metropolitan areas like a Poughkeepsie mall. Alex would be willing to bet the serial killer still lurked somewhere near Wicket Hollow, keeping an eye out for signs of Lyssa. At least while he was so occupied, no other women's lives would be in jeopardy.

Yet.

He could only hope that as long as the Bone Man believed Lyssa to be his immortal mate, no one else would be attacked.

Damn it.

"Alex, are you there?" Trask sounded tired, frus-

trated. Alex couldn't blame him. Being SAC and at war
with the local uniforms was never fun.

"Just thinking. No way in hell he could have made it
all the way to Poughkeepsie. He just burned Lyssa's place."

"I know."

"Keep me posted. Let me know if you find out anything else."

"Will do. Where are you?" Trask sounded suspi-
cious. "Not anywhere near Poughkeepsie are you? Just
on the off chance it is him, you understand."

Alex laughed. "Not even close. Don't worry, I look
after my own." He felt an odd tingling of premonition
as he said it.

"Never doubted that. But be careful. This guy is only
going to get more vicious."

"You don't have to tell me." Closing the phone, Alex
leaned on the porch railing, inhaling the scent of the
rosebushes as he stared into the shadowy woods surrounding the house. From inside, he could hear low
voices as Elaine tried to draw Lyssa out of her shell.

He supposed it was inevitable there would be copycats. Always happened. Some nutcase heard about the
serial killer on the news and decided to try to emulate
him. The reason was anyone's guess.

But copycat it was. Had to be. Alex would bet money
on that. The real Bone Man needed to be brought down,
before anyone else got hurt.

After the phone call with Trask, Alex's adrenaline ran
high. Part of him, the small, secret, savage part, wanted
to climb in his car and roar off to begin his own hunt.
If he could only figure out a way to get Lyssa to agree
to stay with his aunt, he'd actually go.

The screen door swung open and Lyssa stepped outside, holding an unhappy Sam in her arms. Her emerald gaze met his. Again he felt that familiar jolt.

"What did he say?"

"Some copycat attacked a girl at a mall in Poughkeepsie."

She frowned. "What do you mean?"

In a few words he outlined the scenario, ending with his suspicion that this was a imitator.

"You're right," she said, surprising him. "All of the Bone Man's attacks have been in the Catskills. Like he has some sort of connection there."

"I think he's still in Wicket Hollow."

She raised a brow. "Looking for me?"

"Yes. Something about you—maybe just the fact that you got away, seems to have convinced him that you're the one he wants."

For a moment she bowed her head, lost in thought. He studied the graceful lines of her throat, the curve of her spine, and knew a fierce longing to touch her.

To distract himself, he resumed his study of the inviting woods.

"Alex?" When she lifted her gaze to his, he read both curiosity and pain in her expression. "If I colored my hair brunette, would that make a difference?"

He didn't pretend to misunderstand. "No, I don't think so. He already knows you fit his profile. He'll go partly by sight, but more by scent."

"It was worth a shot. Anything that would make a difference and get him off my back." Her attempt to smile fell flat.

Though the wistfulness in her expression made his chest ache, he thought it best to change the subject. "Where's Elaine?"

"She said she'd fixed us something to eat and needed to get it on the table. I asked her if she wanted any help, but she said she worked better alone. She wanted to keep Sam with her, but I'm still a little nervous. She seems to like him, though. A lot."

He nodded. "What about Sam?" The animal regarded him through slitted eyes, ears flat against his head.

She smiled down at her pet. "He's fine—when we're not around you. He likes your aunt, too. She said I could put him in the guest bedroom. I will in a minute, as soon as I set him up with a litter box."

"The guest bedroom?"

"Yes. The one—" she cast him a meaningful look "—with the queen-size bed for us both to sleep in, seeing how we're a married couple and all."

Alex couldn't hide his grin. "Do you want me to tell her differently? I can only imagine the firestorm that would erupt if I told her we wanted separate rooms."

"No, she thinks we're married. And married people share a bed." She looked away. "Remember what happened back at the Hell Hole."

Instantly he sobered. "I remember." Being with her had been his only spot of salvation in the long time working undercover with Hades Claws.

Being with her now—not a good idea. He knew himself well enough to know he could never resist the temptation of sleeping next to her warm, smooth body.

Focus.

"We've shared a bed before." He shrugged, as though it were no big deal, when in reality, as long as he lived, he'd never forget those nights.

Her pupils dilated and he knew she remembered, too.

"That was a mistake." Her lips compressed in a bleak line.

"Big mistake," he agreed.

This time she didn't look away. "No more lies, remember? Ever since I saw you change—"

The screen door opened, slamming back against the house.

"Are you two arguing?" Hands on her ample hips, Elaine looked from Alex to Lyssa and back again.

Alex clenched his jaw. "Just talking. How much did you hear?"

Elaine didn't back down. "Plenty. I heard you two don't want to share a bed."

With difficulty, Alex kept himself from groaning out loud. This was not what he wanted spread all over Leaning Tree. "We had a small disagreement. We'll make up before bedtime."

"Please." Lyssa reached out and touched the older woman's arm. "This is between Alex and me. Could you please…"

"Keep it under my hat?" Her triple chin quivered.

"I was going to say give us some privacy."

"I also heard—" Elaine looked directly at Alex "—that she saw you change. If Lyssa is important to you, that's fine. If not, then you've broken the law."

"The law?" Lyssa echoed, dividing her attention between Elaine and him. She frowned. "He had a good reason to show me. Actually, there is—"

"Lyssa." His one-word warning stopped her. If she told Elaine about the Bone Man before he got a chance to speak with the council, mass panic would result. "Lyssa *is* important to me, Aunt Elaine."

"Are you two really married?"

"Yes." Alex bit out the answer. "We got married three years ago."

"Three years?"

"But we've been separated," Lyssa put in. "For at least half of that time."

"Not by choice." Alex saw Lyssa's eyes widen as she took in the full implication of his words.

"What else?" Eyes alight with curiosity, Elaine folded her arms. "What are you two hiding?"

"You know I'm DEA." He kept his voice low, his tone light. "That information will have to remain classified for now, at least until I speak to the council."

Elaine gasped. "The council? It's that important?"

"It's that important." Sniffing the air, he made a concerted effort to change Elaine's focus. She was like a bloodhound after a scent once she latched on to something. "Did I hear something about you fixing us dinner?"

"Yes." She still squinted at him with suspicion.

"Great." He made a show of rubbing his hands together in anticipation. "I don't know about you, but I'm starving."

Elaine glanced toward Lyssa, who shook her head.

"I'm not all that hungry." She put her hand flat against her stomach. "I'm feeling a little queasy, actually."

This was all Elaine needed to hear. "Honey, a good meal will do you wonders. Ever since Alex told me you were coming, I've been cooking. I've made a nice meal for you two. It's ready, I only need to finish getting it on the table." She bustled into the house, leaving them alone again.

Staring after her, Lyssa swallowed.

"Are you sure you're okay?"

"I'll be fine." She shook her head, as if she needed to clear it. "I've got to feed Sam first." Flipping her hair, she smiled at him over her shoulder as she reached for the door.

Her smile took his breath away.

Frozen, Alex couldn't move. For the space of one heartbeat, then another, he stood rooted to the porch after Lyssa vanished inside, wondering what the hell was wrong with him.

"Alex? Are you coming?" Elaine's voice, still high-pitched with curiosity, brought him out of his trance. He shook his head, glancing once more around the tranquil forest, forcing himself like never before to think about the lure of damp earth and shadowy woods. He thought of the change, waiting for the familiar rush to fill his blood, but all he could see was the beauty of Lyssa's smile. Finally he gave up and went inside.

As he'd predicted, Elaine had prepared a feast. The table groaned under the weight of the food. She'd cooked a whole chicken, plump and golden, as well as a gravy-covered roast. There were new potatoes swimming in butter, freshly shelled peas, and a huge bowl of banana pudding complete with whipped cream.

Lyssa looked at the floor. Though his own mouth watered, he wondered if the scent of the meat turned her stomach. He hadn't had a chance to mention her vegetarian status to Elaine. Now it would be a little awkward.

"Dig in." Determinedly cheerful, his aunt waved a plump arm at his wife and at the food.

Alex pulled out a chair for Lyssa, letting his hand brush her shoulder as she sat.

This time she didn't flinch. As he took his own seat, he wondered why not.

Elaine passed Lyssa the roast. Lyssa handed the platter right over to him.

Two lines appeared between Aunt Elaine's eyebrows.

She passed Lyssa the chicken. Lyssa set it down on the table in front of Alex, making a choking sound.

"Restroom?" she gasped. When Elaine pointed toward the hall, Lyssa sprinted off, slamming the door behind her.

"What's wrong with her?" Still frowning and blunt as always, Aunt Elaine waved a glittering hand at her repast.

Alex sighed. He'd known he'd have to tell her sooner or later. May as well get it over with now.

"She doesn't eat meat."

Elaine narrowed her eyes. "Doesn't eat—you're kidding, right?" Before he could answer, she steamrolled on. "Food used to affect me like that when I was carrying your cousin. Maybe she's pregnant."

Gaping at her, Alex shook his head. *Pregnant?* They'd last made love the weekend of Claire's funeral, nearly three months ago. "She can't be pregnant."

Aunt Elaine watched him, a half smile on her broad face. Waiting.

"Seriously, she's not pregnant. Just look at her."

"Most women don't show with their first until about four months."

Lyssa emerged from the bathroom, pale and shaken. Alex studied her as she crossed the room to her chair, looking for some telltale hint, the slightest bulge, something.

But her loose T-shirt hid her shape. He'd have to run his hand along the curve of her hip, lay the palm of his hand flat against the warmth of her little stomach, to know if her figure had changed from his memories.

Pregnant. No way. Still reeling from the idea, he gave another shake of his head. More likely having two platters of meat shoved at her had turned her stomach.

Lyssa noticed him watching her. "What's wrong?"

"Nothing." He wasn't about to open that can of worms.

Aunt Elaine however, had no such reservations.

"Are you carrying, hon?" she asked.

"Carrying?" Lyssa slid into her chair, assiduously avoiding even glancing at the food. "What do you mean?"

"A baby." Elaine wagged her finger. "Morning sickness affected me like that when I was pregnant."

"Morning—no." Automatically shaking her head, Lyssa looked at him and her green eyes widened. Alex saw the moment when she realized the full implications of such a thing, and he felt it spread like a coldness in his chest.

Bad enough that he was a monster. Now she might be carrying one.

Blindly he reached for his glass, letting the cool slide of water fill his throat. When they'd last made love, Lyssa hadn't known. He hadn't played fair. Yet another rule he'd broken. But he'd made sure she'd been protected. He'd worn a condom.

Lyssa gave Elaine a calm smile. Like him, she pretended to a serenity she didn't feel. Only Alex noticed the way she clasped her hands together tightly, betraying her frayed nerves.

"Pregnant?" She gave a little laugh, utterly false. "No, I'm not."

Alex's heart thudded once, twice. He closed his eyes, gathering his strength, before opening them again to find Lyssa's watching him.

"Are you sure?" Elaine leaned forward.

While Lyssa sat, frozen, glancing from him to Elaine, quick, birdlike little looks—shell-shocked most likely—Elaine moved in for the kill. "How long since your last, you know, *monthly?*"

Instead of answering, Lyssa stared at him. He would have expected to see accusation or something, anything but the blank, utterly emotionless expression she wore. So pale the freckles that dusted her nose stood out, her mouth worked as she tried to speak. "I—"

Swallowing, she made a concentrated effort to try again. "I fainted at the police station. I've never fainted before in my life."

Alex froze. Though he'd used protection, there was always the chance....

"You're carrying," Aunt Elaine crowed. If she'd been with one of her sisters, Aunt Agatha or Aunt Crystal, Alex had no doubt she'd have performed a high five. As it was, he felt the urgent need to get away, before she started congratulating them or choosing baby names.

"Pregnant." A voice echoed, and Alex dimly realized he had spoken out loud. "Pregnant."

"I can't be." Lyssa's protest sounded shaky. A quick look revealed she had her arms crossed defensively and her chin up. "As a matter of fact, I'm positive I'm not."

"Answer her question." Because his own heart had started to pound and his throat had gone bone dry, Alex needed to know now. "How long since your last—?"

"Three months." Her expression was resolute. "But I'm not pregnant. You wore protection, you know. And I did a home pregnancy test. Three of them actually, all different brands. They all were negative. I'm not pregnant. It's stress!"

Nodding, he supposed he should feel relieved. Instead he felt numb.

"Home pregnancy tests are worthless on our kind. You may be human, but your baby's half shifter." Elaine rubbed her hands together. "I just know you're preggers—I have a sense about these things. You'll have to patch things up, for the sake of the baby. Wait until I tell the family."

She grabbed the roast, shoving it in front of Lyssa. "Eat up, mama. Any child of Alex's is sure to need red meat."

With a low cry, Lyssa shoved the plate away. Pushing back her chair so hard it crashed to the floor, she ran again to the bathroom. This time she slammed the door.

Aunt Elaine turned to look at him. "Did you know about this?"

"About the possibility of pregnancy? No." Though he knew any attempt at reason would be met with resistance, he had to try. "Aunt Elaine, you heard Lyssa. She's not pregnant. Home pregnancy tests are the same things the doctors use these days. They're pretty accurate."

"No they're not. Not for us. You really can't be certain. Not until she sees a doctor."

Fine, he'd allow that much. "Until then, I don't think you should call anyone."

"Oh pffft." Elaine pooh-poohed that sentiment. "Any midwife worth her salt could tell you that one's carrying. But I wasn't talking about that. You've got another problem. I'm talking about the way she doesn't eat meat. Did you know about that?"

Typical Aunt Elaine. Faced with any opposition, her favorite tactic was to avoid the issue and do what she damn well pleased. Knowing to resist would be futile and frustrating, he went with the flow.

"That she's a vegetarian? Yes."

"How the hell can a vegetarian marry a—?"

Alex shrugged. "I don't think it matters."

"Not matter?" Elaine came up out of her chair. "Your child is going to need red meat. You can't let her starve the poor pup."

That did it. Pushing himself out of his chair, he strode over and knocked on the bathroom door. Aunt Elaine's gaze tracked him.

"Are you all right?"

"Fine." He heard the sound of water running. He could imagine her splashing her face, the droplets running down her slender throat. At the image, he knew another strong urge to press his mouth against her, to taste the water as he scented her body.

Pregnant. Not once had the possibility even remotely occurred to him. Nor, judging from Lyssa's frantic reaction, had it occurred to her. Though how a woman could miss three months of—

The door swung open.

"Stress," she hissed, as if he'd spoken the question out loud. "My body's messed up because of stress. I mean, I had to stay with a motorcycle gang, I lost my sister...."

He nodded, feeling himself go on automatic pilot. They would both need time to digest this possibility.

"You used a condom."

"I know." Closing his eyes, he swallowed. Opening them, he did what he'd always done to get through. Made a decision. "I want you to see a doctor."

She searched his face. Then nodded. "Okay." Courageously she lifted her chin. "Here?"

"Here, or somewhere. We need to know for certain before we go jumping to conclusions."

In the kitchen he could hear Aunt Elaine on the phone. No doubt the entire family would soon know the news.

"Alex?" Lyssa touched his arm. "I'd really like to get out of here. Maybe go outside for a walk?"

He thought longingly of his untouched plate but nodded. She still looked pale, so maybe fresh air would help.

"Come on. We'll walk down to the town square."

He waved at Aunt Elaine as they went past. Without a break in her phone chatter, she lifted her hand and shooed them out the door. She must be ecstatic with her gossip to let all the food she'd prepared go uneaten.

The screen door squealed as he pushed it open. They stepped out onto the porch and Lyssa pointed to one of the white wooden rockers.

"I used to have one of those in my garden. One of my favorite things was to sit outside in the morning with a mug of fresh coffee and watch the sun rise." She frowned. "I imagine that chair's gone, too, if the fire was as bad as Trask said."

He didn't answer, scenting for trouble. Taking the porch steps slowly, he found nothing abnormal. No signs of trouble.

Outside, the late-afternoon sun dappled the ground as they strolled under huge, leafy oaks.

"Ah." Lyssa inhaled, visibly relaxing. "I love springtime. Nothing like sun on your skin and the smell of fresh-cut lawns and spring flowers."

At the corner of Fifth and Witchtree, they turned right.

Here, the stately houses were larger, more ornate. Brick and elaborate stonework replaced the pastel woods of his aunt's street.

"Beautiful." Lyssa turned shining eyes his way, smiling with pleasure. Her color had returned and she actually had a little bounce in her step.

Staring down into her heart-shaped face, he wanted to bend down and kiss her. Hard, possessively, the kind of kiss that promised more later. But he'd given his word; hands off, so for now he'd have to be content with the sight and scent of her.

For now.

Focus. He had a feeling he'd be using that word a lot around her. He suddenly felt tired. His coveted "adventurous" lifestyle got old sometimes.

"This town is really quiet." Her smile faded and she looked away. "Except for the occasional car going past, it almost feels deserted."

He laughed, having noticed yet another face peeking out from behind lace-trimmed curtains. "It's dinnertime. Once they've all eaten, you'll see hordes of kids playing in front of their houses. Other couples will go for strolls, and their parents will come out and sit on their porches."

He didn't add the other, less desirable fact of small town life—that with every phone call his aunt made, more and more of their neighbors would be watching and wondering. Lyssa'd find out soon enough.

As they crossed Sowell Lane, the residential homes gave way to well-maintained brick businesses. Here, a few stragglers remained, hurrying to their cars after a long day at work, or strolling down to Paddy's for a tall cool one before heading home.

"Looks like he knows you." A tall man headed toward them with a purposeful stride.

Alex felt a knot form in his stomach. He'd left a message at the council's emergency number. Still, he hadn't expected the contact to be so public.

"Lyssa, you're about to meet Frank Mahoney." He took her arm, meaning to give her support and, surprisingly, drawing his own from her. "He's the mayor of Leaning Tree and head of the local council."

Chapter 9

Head of the local council? Lyssa froze, remembering that he, like Aunt Elaine and Alex, was also a shapeshifter.

As he drew nearer, she studied him. An older man, his steel-gray hair was cut short, in an almost military style. But his tanned face seemed friendly, and he broke into a wide smile when he reached them.

"I heard you were in town." Though he spoke to Alex, he openly studied Lyssa. "And that you got married. Congratulations."

"Aunt Elaine's been busy." Though he kept his tone light, Lyssa heard Alex's annoyance. "Frank Mahoney, Lyssa Lupe."

Frank held out his hand. After the tiniest hesitation, Lyssa took it. His clasp felt firm, his large hand warm and...normal. He reminded her of one of her own uncles, friendly and harmless. She tried not to wonder what he'd look like as a wolf.

As though he knew her thoughts, his grin widened as he released her hand.

"Pleased to meet you, pretty lady." His brown eyes twinkled. "Alex, you done good."

"Thanks." Alex moved closer, speaking quietly. "Frank, I need to talk to the entire council. Call an emergency meeting."

Instantly the other man sobered. Searching Alex's face, he gave a slow nod. "When?"

"Tonight, if you can arrange it."

Surprise flickered across Frank's face. "Is it that urgent? I got your message, but I thought—"

"Yes."

"What's this all about?"

Alex glanced at Lyssa, slowly shaking his head. "Long story. Better I tell it once, to the entire council."

"I see." Now even Frank's bearing appeared military. Back ramrod straight, he might have been a general about to call his troops to battle. "Be there at eight o'clock. City hall. I'll call the others." Dipping his head at Lyssa, he moved off.

Lyssa watched him stride away before glancing at Alex. Where before the afternoon had seemed ordinary and relaxing, now she felt Alex's tension vibrating like the pressure drop in the air right before a storm.

"I'm glad that's settled." Though he spoke lightly, he'd jammed his hands in his pockets. The instant she noticed this, he pulled them free.

"Come on." He took her arm. "Once we cross the square, we'll be in another neighborhood. There's someone else I'd like you to meet."

They went two blocks before he stopped in front of a well-maintained older home. A one-story bungalow painted a soft shade of cream, it sat back from the sidewalk on a wide, manicured lawn. With her gardener's eye, Lyssa approved the healthy, trimmed hedges and riot of color from the bright yellow daffodils and multicolored tulips that decorated several brick-edged beds.

"Well done," she said, almost to herself. "Whoever planted this yard takes good care of it. Gardens always reflect such love and effort."

Alex grinned, a mischievous look on his handsome face. Her heart constricted as she stared, unable to look away even though she feared her longing showed in her eyes.

Bad enough she'd realized after Claire's funeral that he could never be the type of man she wanted. A daredevil, Alex lived for the risk taking, the adrenaline rush. He loved his undercover work, the danger, the thrill. He could never be the kind of husband content to live the ordinary life she craved—raising kids and plants and becoming involved in her small town. Bad enough she'd had to accept this and let him go, but now she'd learned he was a werewolf. Yet even now, knowing what he was, what he could become, she found herself drawn to him. Even now, she still wanted him.

His grin ebbed slowly away as he returned her stare. Heat flared in his gaze. Intent, he took a step closer, reminding her of a hunter tracking prey. She lifted her hand to her throat, but stood her ground.

"Alex!" a laughing voice called. "I can't believe you're back!"

A slender woman, her auburn hair in a long, fat braid down her back, stood poised on the porch. Sleek and graceful, she reminded Lyssa of an exotic, well-groomed animal. Despite her darker hair, the resemblance between her and Alex was unmistakable.

"Come on." Alex put his arm around her, propelling her forward. "Lyssa, meet my sister, Brenna. Brenna, this is my wife."

Brenna gave another glad cry and launched herself at them. Enveloping both Lyssa and Alex in a perfumed hug, she laughed. "You can't know how thrilled I am to meet you."

"What about me?" Another voice, baritone and throaty, spoke from the doorway. Lyssa stared. She'd met the dark-haired man with his rugged features once before, when she'd first joined Hades Claws.

"Carson." Pivoting on the balls of her feet, Brenna spun. "Come meet Alex's wife."

"We've already met." Unsmiling, he descended the steps. "Though it was nearly two years ago and you probably don't remember me."

"I remember."

Carson nodded. "Another place and another time." He went to his wife, putting his arm protectively around her shoulders.

Caramel eyes glowing, Brenna placed both hands on her abdomen, pulling her oversized T-shirt tight to showcase her gently rounded shape. "We have news!"

"You're pregnant?" Surprise echoed in Alex's voice.

Brenna and Carson looked at each other, both breaking out in identical grins. The love they shared was obvious.

"Yes. Baby's due in five months." The joy in her voice was unmistakable. Lyssa found herself wondering what it would be like, to share such love, to have such a joyous hope for the future. A real marriage, two people soon to become three. A family. Her greatest desire.

Another round of hugs and exclamations increased Lyssa's absurd feeling of loss. Seeing Brenna and Carson, she couldn't help but compare to herself and Alex. Doing so only made her feel bereft, without hope. To her dismay, she felt that familiar ache in the back of her throat, the sting of tears starting in her eyes.

But then Alex turned and held out his hand.

Feeling everyone's gaze upon her, Lyssa gingerly reached out and slid her fingers into his big hand, finding his touch both familiar and comforting.

When he turned to face the others, his expression had once again gone impassive, his undercover face. Even with his sister... "We've got problems." He squeezed Lyssa's hand, surprising her. "I'm meeting with the council tonight."

"Come inside." Her own face turning grave, Brenna plucked at her brother's arm. "Carson told me a bit about your troubles."

Carson shook his dark head. "Knowing Alex, I'm sure what little I know is just the tip of the iceberg."

They all trooped up the steps and inside the ornate wooden door. Again, watching the loving interaction between Brenna and Carson gave Lyssa a curious swooping feeling in her stomach, though this time for a different reason. Carson was human. Brenna was not. How had he adjusted to the fact that he was married to a werewolf? Her gaze slid to Brenna's slightly rounded shape. Never mind that, how had he reconciled himself to the thought that his child might be one also?

She sighed. Had she really believed she might someday be allowed to have a safe and boring life? Ever since her mother had died when Lyssa was sixteen, looking after her wild, younger sister had guaranteed her a thrill a minute. Sure, Lyssa'd continued to strive for serenity—opening the nursery full of comforting green, growing things had been one such attempt. But Claire's penchant for getting in trouble, ending in her violent death, had destroyed Lyssa's fervent hopes that her baby sister would ever settle down.

Maybe, just maybe, once the Bone Man had been stopped, she could rebuild her business and finally find the peaceful existence she'd always longed for.

Without Alex. She didn't need that kind of heartache.

Unfortunately, she knew letting him go this time would hurt just as much or more as the last.

"Lyssa?" Brenna's lilting voice brought her out of her thoughts. "Are you all right?"

"Of course I am." Lyssa smiled. "Why don't you show me the rest of your house? I'd love to see it."

While Brenna showed her the house, Lyssa gave her a quick rundown of the situation, guessing Alex was doing the same with Carson in the other room.

An hour or two later, Lyssa and Alex got ready to take their leave. The afternoon shadows had lengthened and, glancing at her watch, Lyssa was surprised to realize it was nearly seven. "Your meeting is at eight?"

Checking his own watch, Alex winced. "We need to go. I can't be late." He slipped his arm around Lyssa's waist. Brenna and Carson followed as they walked outside.

"Come on, I need to get you back to Elaine's first."

Lyssa stopped. "Then you'd have to come all the

way back downtown. You stay here. I can get to Elaine's by myself."

Arms around each other, Brenna and Carson silently watched them.

Alex looked down at Lyssa. Because his face was in shadow, she couldn't read his expression. "Not a chance." He spoke lightly, but undercurrents of warning echoed in his voice. "I'm not leaving you unprotected."

"I thought you said I was safe here."

"You are. As far as I know. But I don't believe in taking chances."

"We really need to start my weapons training." Lifting her chin, Lyssa gave him her most stern look.

"Weapons training?" Both Brenna and Carson spoke at once, exchanging long looks.

"I've asked Alex to help me learn how to better defend myself. I took a self-defense class, but it wasn't nearly enough."

"I agree," Brenna said, surprising her. "I hate guns myself. I've learned jujitsu, but that wasn't enough either. You can't rely on anyone but yourself when the fur starts flying."

"Hey!" With a look of mock outrage, Carson put his arm around his wife and pulled her close. "You know I'll always protect you."

"I know honey." She kissed him on the cheek, then looked at Lyssa and winked.

Lyssa laughed out loud. Both Carson and Alex stared at her like they thought she'd lost her mind.

"Let's go." Alex slipped his arm around Lyssa's waist. She stiffened, then, noting the other couple's avid interest, relaxed.

They said their goodbyes, promising to stop by again.

Once outside, Lyssa tried to pull free. Grinning, he wouldn't release her.

She stopped. "Let me go. No one can see us now."

"Oh, yes they can." He gestured at the houses on their side of the street. "You can't imagine how far ranging my aunt Elaine's reach can be. Right now I wouldn't be surprised if every house we pass has people watching us from behind their curtains."

She gave up, letting Alex walk her all the way to his aunt's house. Still on the phone, Elaine waved to them as they went past the kitchen. While they'd been gone, she'd cleared the table and no sight of the enormous dinner remained.

Inside the guest bedroom, Sam greeted her with a loud meow, winding himself around her legs. He gave Alex a perfunctory hiss before getting back to the business of welcoming his mama.

"I've got to go." Alex brushed her cheek with the kind of kiss husbands everywhere gave their wives. In *real* marriages, she reminded herself, pushing away the ache.

"Where will you be sleeping?" Swallowing hard, Lyssa lifted her gaze to his.

He had the grace to look embarrassed. "Aunt Elaine only has two bedrooms. Hers and the guestroom."

"Great." She rolled her eyes. "Can't you sleep on the couch?"

"I can. I'd prefer to stay together, but I will, if that's what you want."

Her pulse sped up. She held his gaze for the space of one, two heartbeats, then looked away. "No. I want you with me."

"Fine." He didn't make a big production out of her admission, for which she was eternally grateful.

"Alex, be careful."

"Stay here, ok?"

She nodded, busying herself with pouring Sam the food they'd picked up on the way home into a small plastic bowl. She didn't look up until she heard the front door close.

Once Alex had gone, she breathed a sigh of relief. Time alone was exactly what she needed. Time alone to figure things out.

Though Alex's aunt had placed several magazines on the nightstand, once Lyssa climbed into bed to read, she felt an overwhelming urge to sleep. So she snuggled down under the sheets and did exactly that.

A small sound awakened her. From her feet, Sam growled a warning, ever the watch-cat.

A large shadow filled the doorway, stepping inside and closing the door behind him. Alex. Watching him from under her lashes, her breath caught as he began to shed his clothes. The dim moonlight that came through the blinds bathed him in an otherworldly glow as he removed his shirt and stepped out of his jeans, wearing only dark-colored boxers.

The bed dipped when he climbed in beside her. Lyssa held absolutely still, afraid even to inhale. Her heart pounded, seeming so loud she feared he would hear.

But he said nothing, stretching out on top of the covers like a large, well-fed cat, displacing Sam, who made his displeasure known with a hiss and a yowl.

Alex knew she was awake—she'd bet on it.

He rolled onto his back. She could barely make out his rugged profile in the muted light from the streetlight outside.

Neither spoke. She could hear him breathing, knew

he could tell she wasn't asleep from her own uneven breaths.

"How'd it go?" She finally had to ask, rolling to her other side so she could face him.

"I outlined the threat, including the potential for something to go wrong. I even gave them several options for action."

She propped herself up on one elbow. "Did they decide on anything?"

"Our council acts like politicians anywhere." He sounded weary. "They argued and debated. Most believed me—a few did not. Some of them wanted proof the serial killer is one of us, a shape-shifter."

"Proof? How'd they think you'd be able to get that?"

"Who knows? But how else would the Bone Man know about the legend of King Nebeshed? I think that's what finally decided them, though a couple of them still felt I was too close to the issue." He sighed. "Maybe they're right about that. But they finally voted and agreed the Bone Man has to be stopped, just in case."

"Did they have any ideas how?"

He gave a quiet chuckle, the low, masculine rumble causing her insides to do somersaults. "Not really. But they want me to take care of him personally. Which is no less than I expected."

The kill is mine. Where had that thought come from? Lyssa bit her lip to keep from gasping. Yet, though she knew Alex hadn't spoken, she'd heard the words as clearly as if he'd shouted them.

"The kill is…yours?" Hesitant to ask, she did anyway. She had to know if she'd really heard his thoughts so clearly or if it had been only her imagination.

A major one.

She needed to sleep. She closed her eyes, trying to think calming thoughts. Yet the silence seemed to amplify his closeness rather than muffle it.

"This is uncomfortable." She gave in to the urge to pound her pillow. "Maybe you really should sleep on the couch."

He got up and swung his legs over the side of the bed, his back ramrod straight.

"Wait." She touched his arm. "Doesn't this bother you?"

He didn't pretend to misunderstand. "You're asking me if I mind lying next to you, inches away, with the scent of your desire filling my lungs? I can see the outline of your shape, and my hands remember the feel of your soft skin, the curve of your hip, the swell of your breast." With each word his voice seemed to grow more hoarse. "Yes, this bothers me."

Meltdown. Her body suffused with heat, she was temporarily speechless. His words had brought to mind the way he'd always touched her, like she was something infinitely precious, and the fire that blazed between them.

They'd burned together.... No!

He sat up and grabbed his pillow. "Your thoughts..."

That damned connection again. She felt her face heat. Did he mean he knew exactly what she'd been thinking? *Crap.*

The mattress creaked as he pushed himself to his feet.

"What are you doing?"

"Moving to the floor." Though husky, his tone was excruciatingly polite. "I don't suppose you'd mind if I took the comforter for my bed?"

"Stop it," she snapped. "You can stay. We're both adults. We can handle this."

"Yes, we can." His immediate agreement made her wince. If he was channeling her blatantly sexual thoughts, evidently they didn't affect him as strongly as they did her.

The bed dipped as he lay back down. Restless, she scooted a bit closer to the edge on her side. Away from him.

He chuckled, low in his throat. "This is ridiculous."

Lyssa couldn't help but shiver. The urge to touch him felt almost overpowering. Almost. Biting down on the inside of one cheek, she rolled over onto her other side instead. Maybe with her back to him they could both get some sleep.

And avoid touching each other. Touching each other would be a bad mistake. Infernos ignited when they touched, universes exploded when they kissed. How well she remembered... Ruthlessly, she cut off the thought. Sleep. She needed to think about sleep.

"I feel it too, you know." This time Alex sounded like a man in pain. She suddenly realized, as clearly as if she could feel him, that he was hard and aroused.

Ready.

Ah, damn. She closed her eyes, trying not to remember how he'd felt buried deep inside her, how he'd filled her and made her feel so much more than pleasure.

She was in trouble.

"Me too," he said. "Deep trouble." His voice shook. Had she spoken out loud?

Though he hadn't moved, she swore she could feel the heat of his breath on the back of neck. Imagination. Had to be. Much like the sensual memories that made her long to roll over, scoot across the bed, and press her aching breasts into his chest. Or guide his hand to her swollen nipples, or his mouth or...

She groaned. "This isn't working."

"No joke." He reached out his hand, then let it drop to the mattress between them. "I want you, Lyssa."

Honesty. Damn. "I want you too, Alex. But we shouldn't. We can't. We need to focus."

For all her brave words, she lied. She knew that and he knew it as well. All she wanted to focus on was him—the beauty of his touch, the sweet oblivion making love with him would bring. Her heart pounded and she couldn't catch her breath. If she didn't put an end to this now, they'd soon be going at it with the same wonderful, mindless passion that had helped her blot out the pain of her sister's death.

As if great sex could chase away sorrow or fear.

"Focus." Alex spoke the word bitterly, like a curse. "For the first time in my life I've lost my focus. I can't think straight when you're around."

Like scratching an itch. He'd made no secret of what she meant to him. And, just like the Monday after Claire's funeral, he'd love her and leave her and break her heart again.

"One of us has to!" Determined this time to be stronger, she rolled off the bed to her feet. Legs shaky, she forced herself to move away from him. She went to the dresser and, groping blindly in the dim light, grabbed her hairbrush.

He didn't come after her. Part of her was disappointed. She couldn't even take comfort in the fact that she was right and he knew it.

Dragging the brush through her hair, she concentrated on the feel of the bristles on her scalp and slowing her erratic heartbeat.

On the other side of the bed, the guest bathroom doorway beckoned like a beacon to safety. Moving fast, before she gave in to temptation, Lyssa rushed around the bed, into the bathroom, and closed the door behind her before she flicked on the light.

She should have felt safe. But her own body betrayed her. The sight of herself in the mirror reinforced that. Her pupils were dilated, dark with smoky desire. Her nipples showed against her T-shirt, and the aching heat pulsing in her body made her bite her lip to keep from moaning.

Damn she wanted him. But she couldn't. She wouldn't. Reaching for the faucet to splash cold water on her face, she looked at the shower and had a better idea.

A cold shower. To keep herself from taking advantage of the temptation in the other room. A hot, late spring night and a tempting man. She shook her head. What was wrong with her? Most women would think they were in paradise, even if he was the love-'em-and-leave-'em type.

But then most women weren't married to a werewolf.

Stripping off her long T-shirt, Lyssa turned the water on cold and stepped inside the shower. The icy water felt invigorating—no, it didn't. Who was she kidding? She was *freezing*. Like everyone else, she'd always heard of men taking cold showers to cool their libido, but this was ridiculous.

Shivering, she turned the knob, bringing in more hot water until the spray was a comfortable temperature. She reached for the soap, lathering herself and trying not to think of Alex stretched out on the bed, waiting.

But her aroused body had other ideas. The rough texture of the soapy washcloth, the glide of the soap on her skin, even the spray of water changed and became sensual things.

In the other room waited the one man who could give her what her body so desperately wanted. Sex. Raw, hot, sex. Her only problem was that she didn't know how to indulge her body without engaging her mind. Still, knowing this didn't erase her need for release. This felt more and more urgent, compounding her frustration.

What the hell. With a small, savage smile, Lyssa closed her eyes, letting the wet washcloth become something else, something or someone she wanted more than was safe or prudent.

She let her thoughts go, let her wildest fantasies, her most secret dreams play out. Alex. If only...

"I'm here."

With a gasp, Lyssa opened her eyes. Naked, his splendid body fully aroused, Alex stood framed by the shower curtain. Eyes dark, he took the soapy cloth from her suddenly boneless fingers.

"Lyssa, I *feel* you." His deep voice sounded hoarse. "I feel your fire, your heat, your need. For me. As fierce as my own for you. I can't focus, can't think, on anything but this."

Still holding himself away from her, he drew the washcloth across her skin, cupping her aching breasts with a reverence that only increased her desire tenfold.

Suddenly her concerns seemed a hundred times less important than they had a moment ago. Human or werewolf, this was Alex. Her Alex, her husband, the man she was, despite herself, growing to trust. Alex. Hard and muscular, sleek and fierce.

They had no real future together. Once the Bone Man was gone, they'd each resume their separate lives.

Ah, but God help her, had any woman ever wanted a man so much?

"May I?" He asked her permission to join her.

She inhaled, letting him see the force of her desire in her eyes. "Yes."

He stepped inside the shower, pulling the curtain closed behind him.

She wanted to touch him, stroke him, feel the length of him filling her. But she did none of those things—instead she merely *thought* them, watching Alex's face as her thoughts communicated themselves to him.

"Hellhounds, Lyssa." He pulled her to him, soap and all. Their slick skin still burned despite the less than scalding water and she fancied they made steam.

He slipped inside her, the fit perfect, filling her—exactly as she'd remembered him. Head back, she let her eyes drift closed. Not thinking, not analyzing, feeling nothing but sensation as Alex began to move.

Chapter 10

Toweling off, Alex watched Lyssa carefully for some sign of regret. All he could sense from her was fulfilled satisfaction, similar to his own. That and an overwhelming contentment.

Had she finally realized they could have a future, once she came to terms with his dual nature? Would such a thing be too much to hope for so soon?

One thing for sure, they had friggin' little time to work out their complicated emotions. Until they brought the Bone Man down, finding and eliminating the serial killer was all Alex could afford to focus on.

The council had given him a week.

Focus. He had to regain his focus.

For the first time since beginning his career as a DEA agent, Alex felt worried. A week to locate and take down a crazed madman? But the council was right. The

Bone Man had to be stopped before he killed again. Alex had been thinking only of Lyssa. Since the serial killer had seemed fixated on her, Alex had pushed away the worry for any other women. That wasn't like him at all.

But no one knew the mind of a psychopath. Alex couldn't guarantee the Bone Man wouldn't torture a few more women along the way with his bizarre testing.

"Alex?" Lyssa's tentative voice broke his reverie. Turning, he couldn't help but admire her lithe body as she stood in front of him, unembarrassed. She turned sideways, studying herself in the mirror. "See?"

He felt his smile widen. "I like what I see. A lot."

Shooting him a stern look, she tried for a frown but was unable to keep from smiling, even as she shook her head. "Alex, I'm serious. I'm talking about my shape." She splayed her hands across her abdomen. "Here. Totally flat. Not even a hint of rounding. No way am I pregnant."

On impulse he pulled her up against him and kissed her, long and deep and full of promise. Though he was exhausted, to his disbelief his body quickened again.

Judging from Lyssa's quick catch of breath, she felt it, too. "Alex…" Her protest was mixed with amusement. "This is important. Despite the fact that you used a condom, despite the negative home pregnancy tests, I need to be sure."

"I have to point this out—"

Holding up her hand, she cut him off. "I know. We took a chance just now in the shower. A big chance."

"I refuse to apologize, not for that. We are married."

Her expression became weary. "I know. So even if I wasn't pregnant before, I could be now. But your Aunt

Elaine's comments have me worried. I believed the home pregnancy tests before. I didn't know all the other stuff, especially the shifter thing. I need to know for sure."

"You're right." Reluctantly, he turned away, snugging the towel more securely around his waist. "Though I agree it's unlikely you're pregnant, you have missed three months. I think you should get checked."

"I will." She sounded very uncertain, so lost he wanted to kiss her. "Tomorrow. We'll find a doctor in town."

"Yoo-hoo?" Aunt Elaine called out, her cheery voice followed by three sharp taps on the bathroom door. "Is everything all right in there?"

"Oh my God," Lyssa muttered, turning three shades of crimson. "I can't believe…"

"She didn't hear anything. Maybe the shower, but that's about it. We were quiet." He raised his voice. "We're fine, Aunt Elaine."

"Good." She chuckled. "I'm going for a run in the woods."

Lyssa's eyes widened. "Is she…?"

"Most likely." Though he managed any inflection from his voice, Alex watched her closely. Her reaction to the idea of Aunt Elaine changing to a wolf would help him gauge her level of acceptance.

Lyssa held his gaze. She swallowed, then gave him a tentative smile. "Is it fun?"

Her question confused him. "I don't understand. Is what fun?"

"Becoming a wolf. I can't imagine such a thing, though once when I was around six or seven, we went on vacation somewhere in Pennsylvania. I stood in a clearing, looking out over rolling meadows of green, and wished I could become a doe so I could run. Unfettered. Free." She sighed, her expression wistful. "Does changing into a wolf feel something like that?"

A sharp joy stabbed him, so fierce he wanted to kiss her senseless. No longer afraid or repulsed, now she was trying to understand.

"It's fun." Then, because the simple answer wasn't enough, he elaborated. "Being a wolf feels like I'm pure muscle and sinew and power. When I become the animal, every breath I take, every beat of my heart, is part of the earth." He gave her a savage grin, wishing he had better words to describe it.

"The earth?"

"Yes. We're all connected. Humans tend to forget this, in their concrete cities and metal cars. But the animals always remember, and when I become my wolf self, I feel the earth's pulse. I feel her breathe under the pads of my feet, and weep in the spring showers." He paused, embarrassed at waxing so poetic.

She blinked. "You love it, don't you?" Her soft voice was full of wonder.

"Sometimes I think my life would be easier if I could stay a wolf." He hadn't meant to sound so bitter.

Watching him, she gave a slow nod. "You've seen things in your line of work that make you want to shun humanity, haven't you?"

Stunned, he stared at her. She understood. No one, except maybe Carson, realized how his job affected him. That was why he'd taken the leave of absence, intending to hang out with Brenna and Carson and try to reconnect with society.

The Bone Man had changed all that. But the crazed

killer had brought Alex back to Lyssa, so they had that much to be grateful for.

"Thank you." He gave into impulse and pulled her into his arms for a quick, fierce hug.

"For what?"

"For being you." His voice sounded rough. Clearing his throat, he planted a kiss on the top of her head. "Come on, let's try and get some sleep. In the morning, I'll need your help—we've got to come up with a plan."

Hand in hand, they left the bathroom. As they slid under the sheets, he was careful not to touch her. She rolled onto her side, curled away from him; he lay on his back, watching her.

"Hold me," she asked, her soft voice drowsy. So he did, moving up behind her so that her bottom nestled snugly against him. He should have been sated, but his body had other ideas. Lyssa sighed and murmured, her deep, even breathing telling him she slept.

He held her, his arousal gradually subsiding. He felt as though he touched something precious and fragile and unique.

In the morning Alex woke to the homey smell of bacon frying. Though he usually had only coffee, his stomach growled.

"Oh, no," Lyssa groaned, burying her face in her pillow. "I'm going to get sick."

"Let me get you some coffee."

"Juice." She made another sound, dragging the sheet over her head. Alex pulled on his boxers, then the jeans he'd let fall to the floor the night before.

In the kitchen, Aunt Elaine transferred another rasher of bacon to the mound on the counter beside her. "I made eggs, too, and sausage," she said happily. "And I can whip up some waffles if you'd like."

He nodded, snatching a handful of bacon from the bottom of the pile as it was less hot. "Right now I need coffee."

She pointed to the cabinet above her coffeemaker. "The cups are in there. Knock yourself out."

He grabbed a mug, then filled a glass with orange juice for Lyssa.

When he reentered the bedroom, Lyssa was nowhere to be found. He glanced at the closed bathroom door and placed her glass on the nightstand.

Behind the door, she retched.

"Are you all right?"

"Fine." She didn't sound fine. Had the smell of the bacon alone made her ill? This reminded him of morning sickness—surely she could see that. He dragged a hand across his jaw, then took a deep drink of coffee.

"I brought you some OJ."

She made a muffled reply that he couldn't decipher. A moment later she emerged from the bathroom, pale and weak. Crossing to the nightstand, she picked up her glass, sniffed it and winced. Carefully replacing it, she looked at Alex and gave him a feeble smile. "I think I need a shower. Go ahead and eat without me. If I can keep anything down, it'll have to be oatmeal or cereal."

Taking another deep draft of his coffee, he tried to figure out how to say it. "Lyssa, you seem to have morning sickness."

"I know." She sighed, running a hand through her already disheveled hair. "Either that or I've picked up a nasty flu."

He let that one go. "After breakfast, we'll see about finding that doctor."

She nodded once before disappearing back into the bathroom and closing the door. A moment later he heard the shower start. He stood a moment longer, staring at the door, before shaking his head.

A hearty meal always cleared his thinking. Alex made his way to the kitchen. Beaming, Aunt Elaine waited. She'd placed several huge serving bowls in the center of the table, one filled with scrambled eggs, the other with hash browns. There was even a smaller bowl of oatmeal. A platter of buttered toast and the pile of bacon completed the repast.

"Did you decide if you wanted waffles? Or pancakes? I have real maple syrup." Her eagerness made him grin.

"I think this is more than enough." He helped himself to a piece of bacon before grabbing a plate. "As usual, you've outdone yourself."

She giggled. "Got to keep up the strength, now don't we?"

Because his mouth was full of bacon, Alex only winked.

"Where's that pretty wife of yours?"

"Taking a shower." He decided not to mention the morning sickness. No sense in stirring that up again.

"I hope she's hungry. I made this oatmeal especially for her. Oh!" Elaine spun, her brightly colored skirt flaring, jewelry jingling. "I nearly forgot the cantaloupe."

When she finally sat down and filled a plate, Alex was working on his second helping. Between the two of them, they made short work of the bacon and eggs, which was good since that meant Lyssa wouldn't have to deal with the sight and scent of them.

"The oatmeal's getting cold," Elaine fretted.

"That's okay." Lyssa rounded the corner, looking much better than she had before. The shower seemed to have energized her. Her eyes sparkled and her fair skin had regained a healthy color.

In fact, he thought suddenly, she glowed. He'd always heard that said about pregnant women. Another reason to think Lyssa carried his child.

"I can microwave it," Elaine offered.

"If you'd point me toward the microwave, I'll zap it myself." Lyssa smiled, grabbing an empty bowl and spooning up oatmeal. "With milk and brown sugar. Thank you so much for making this."

"You're welcome." Elaine pointed Lyssa to the microwave, then bustled around the kitchen, coming up with a tan box sealed inside a Ziploc bag. "Brown sugar!"

"Wonderful." Lyssa glanced at Alex. "I'm starving."

When she sat down, she dug in with gusto. Both Elaine and Alex watched her, Elaine looking satisfied as Lyssa scraped the sides of her bowl with her spoon.

Slung over the back of her chair, Lyssa's purse began to play "Flashdance." She froze in the act of reaching to refill her bowl.

"What's that?" Elaine cocked her head.

"My cell phone." Lyssa's voice came out in a squeak. "I left it on so Marilee could call." Reaching for her purse, she began rummaging inside. "Here it is."

As she triumphantly held up her little flip phone and opened it to answer, the ring-tone song stopped.

"I missed it." She peered at the caller ID screen on the front. "That's odd. I don't recognize the number."

He shrugged. "So it wasn't Marilee. If it's important enough, they'll call back."

"You don't understand. It *had* to be important. No one calls me at this number unless it is."

This he didn't get. "Why not? Why have a cell phone if you don't use it?"

She scrunched up her face. "No minutes. I have the bargain plan. So I only use this phone in emergencies."

Elaine gestured at the table. "Then I guess it'll have to keep," she said brightly. "At least until after you've eaten your second helping."

"Seconds?" Lyssa blanched, still staring at her phone. "No thanks—I'm stuffed. If you two are hungry, go ahead."

"We've already eaten. You on the other hand, might be feeding two. So maybe you should—"

"Aunt Elaine." Alex silenced her with a quick look. "Lyssa needs to check this out. It could be important."

Elaine grumbled, but kept the rest of her comments to herself.

"Thanks." A ghost of a smile touched Lyssa's mouth. "Just wait a minute—it probably went to voice mail."

As though in agreement, the phone beeped.

"Yep. One new voice message."

Shaking her head, Elaine stabbed at the last piece of bacon with a fork. Chewing slowly, she stared while Lyssa retrieved her message.

"Oh my God!" Going pale, Lyssa raised her hand to her mouth. "It's him."

Alex didn't need to ask who she meant. He reached for the phone. "What does he want?"

She swayed, evading him. "He's says it's time to come out and play."

"Right," Alex scoffed, ever conscious of Elaine's avid interest. "Does he really think you are—"

"You don't understand." Lyssa raised tortured eyes to his. "He's got Marilee. He says he'll kill her if we don't do as he asks."

"What?" Elaine stood, pushing away her plate. "What on earth are you two talking about?"

They both ignored her, staring at each other.

"Let me listen." Again Alex reached for the phone. This time Lyssa let him take it.

"Dial one to repeat the message," she said.

As soon as the voice began to speak, Alex felt a chilling premonition.

"I have the other woman, but I don't think Marilee is my queen." Good, that meant she might still be alive.

"There is one way for me to find out. Kill her and take her rib." He laughed, a chilling sound. "If you want her to live, you must come to me and let me test you. Only you, no others. Give yourself up to what is meant to be. Eternal life and power shall be ours." The Bone Man concluded his chilling litany with instructions on where she was to go—an area near Woodstock—and how long he'd wait for her—no more than two or three hours.

"Do you recognize his voice?" Lyssa watched Alex, her expression hopeful.

"No." He dialed the last number on the caller ID screen, hitting Send. The phone on the other end rang. After seventeen rings he disconnected. "No answer. It's probably a pay phone. I'm sure he knows cell numbers can be traced. Still, that's all we've got. It's worth a shot."

Immediately, he began punching in another number.

"What are you doing?" Lyssa snatched the phone away.

He glared at her. "We've got to call Trask."

"No! The Bone Man said not to. I don't want to endanger Marilee."

Aunt Elaine gasped. "The Bone Man? Do you mean that serial killer that's been on the news—the Catskill Killer?"

Great. Just what he needed. "In a minute, Aunt Elaine." He kept his gaze fixed on Lyssa, willing her to understand. "Trask needs to know. He can run a check on the number."

"Alex—"

"What's going on here?" Hands on ample hips, Elaine's tone said she would not be ignored again. "Why on earth is a serial killer calling *you?* Who is Marilee?"

Alex glanced at her, then at Lyssa, who had begun to shake. Delayed reaction.

"We've got to go." Making a quick decision, he pushed back his chair and went to Lyssa, touching her arm. "I'm sorry Aunt Elaine."

"Whoa—hold on! You can't just run out of here without telling me—"

She was right. He had to forewarn her, just in case.

"The Bone Man—the Catskill Killer—is after Lyssa. I brought her up here to hide her from him."

Elaine gasped. "You told this to the council last night?"

"Yes. They are fully aware of the situation."

"Situation?" She narrowed her eyes. "Does he know she's here?"

"No." He swallowed. "I don't think so."

"I see. There's more that you're not telling me, isn't there?"

"It's a Pack decision but yes, I've claimed the kill." The bed dipped as he shifted. "How did you know that?"

"I don't know. I thought I heard you say that."

"Our connection grows stronger." He sounded oddly satisfied. "The longer we're together, the more we bond."

Bond, schmond. She let that one go. "Do you truly plan to kill him? The Bone Man, I mean? You work for law enforcement. Wouldn't it be a better thing, not to mention more legal, to arrest him and let him stand trial?"

"If he were human, yes. But that option is no longer possible." Regret echoed in his voice. "By his actions he endangers the entire Pack. As such, he cannot be allowed to live."

Lyssa had no response for such a statement. She couldn't even fathom his way of thinking. More proof of how large the gulf was between them and their worlds.

But his proximity in the darkened room made their differences hard to remember. This close, she could smell the faint scent of him, masculine and musk. If she leaned forward, she could place her mouth on his bare chest, touch her tongue to his skin and taste him. Instead she kept utterly still, afraid to move. Yet her pulse sped up, unable to push away the erotic thoughts brought on by the way he sprawled next to her, so close his breath tickled her cheek every time he exhaled.

Alex. Desire rose in her, so fierce she clenched her teeth. Though she ached to touch him, she would not. She'd do well to remember that the simmering attraction between them was yet another threat to her quest for serenity.

Good old Aunt Elaine. She'd always been able to see straight through him. He glanced at Lyssa. She had gone to the window and stood with her back to them, staring outside.

"He's one of us," he finally said. "And he believes he's King Nebeshed, returned to life. He kills tall, blond human women because—"

"He's searching for his immortal queen."

"Right."

"Oh my hounds." Elaine lifted her hand to her mouth. "Then he might be on his way here, to Leaning Tree."

Lyssa turned to look at them. "We've got to go." Her quiet voice sounded steady. If not for the way she twisted her hands, he might have thought her calm. "We can't endanger anyone here."

"Come on." He took Lyssa's arm. She let him, though from her subdued movements he thought she might still be in shock. "He won't come here. No one is in danger. He called you because he wants you to come to him. Go to the car, I'll get your things."

Elaine protested. "What are you going to do? Do you have a plan?"

Lyssa strode forward, pushing open the screen door and heading toward his car. Alex ran to the guest room and gathered their things, then ran back to the car. He turned to look at his aunt, who now stood on the porch.

"I'm sorry, Aunt Elaine, but we've got to go. No sense in taking any chances. As soon as we're able, we'll fill you in."

Her blue eyes gleamed. "First?"

"It's a promise." He slid into his car and started the engine.

"Wait." Lyssa scrambled from the car. "I've got to get Sam."

"Let me keep him," Elaine said. "That way he won't be in any danger."

"I don't know…" Lyssa hesitated, clearly torn.

"Please." Her expression earnest, Elaine touched her arm. "I promise I'll take good care of him."

"It'd be safer, not to mention less stressful." Alex waited, watching while Lyssa debated. Finally, she squeezed Elaine's hand and gave a slow nod.

"You swear no harm will come to him?"

Though she couldn't possibly know, she asked of his aunt a solemn oath among their kind.

Elaine's eyes grew misty. "You're a fit wife for my nephew." She said. "Yes, I swear it."

"Then I'll leave him."

Aunt Elaine could scarcely contain her delight. "Alex has my number. You can call anytime and check on him."

"Thank you." Lyssa got into the car without another word, closing the door in a hurry, no doubt before she changed her mind.

"Are you ready now?"

"Yes." Lyssa bit her lip. "More ready than you can imagine. You've got to teach me how to shoot."

"There's no time for that now." He shifted into drive. As they pulled away, he waved. Lyssa echoed his movement halfheartedly.

"We need to make time."

"Okay." He thought of the box of silver bullets the council had given him and debated whether to tell her. "Are you all right?"

"No. Yes." She shook her head, then gave a slow nod. "I want to blow his head off."

"Lyssa."

"I know. But he's got Marilee. I don't understand how the hell that could happen."

Alex couldn't either. How good *was* this guy? First he'd gotten past the local police to trash Lyssa's house, then he'd gone through trained FBI agents to torch it. Now he'd managed to grab Lyssa's best friend, right out from under their noses.

He was either very, very good or very, very lucky.

"How long until we get there?" She meant Woodstock.

"A while." Since he'd promised no more lies, he'd try to dodge answering as long as possible. He didn't plan to take Lyssa anywhere near Woodstock or the Bone Man. He wanted to lock her away in a well-guarded safe house, preferably far away from here. There, even if he had to carry her in kicking and screaming, he could make sure she was protected.

If she hated him afterward, he'd have only himself to blame. At least he wouldn't have to worry about her safety. Once she was taken care of, he could hunt the Bone Man. Alone.

"Why'd you tell your aunt the truth?"

"I had to." He shrugged. "I can't endanger her. Even though she's a shifter and can defend herself, she's old."

She sat up straight. "Endanger her? You think the Bone Man—"

"I don't know what he'd do, Lyssa. Neither do you."

"I wonder how he got my cell-phone number?"

"Yeah, me too. I don't even have that number."

"Maybe he found a cell-phone bill when he was trashing my house before he set it on fire. Or maybe he got it from—" she swallowed "—Marilee."

That made sense. Now, there was the matter of Trask.

Though he wanted Lyssa calm, he couldn't wait too much longer to call him. He needed to find out what exactly was going on.

"Write down your cell number for me." He handed her a slip of paper from his console, waiting while she jotted down the number, then folding the square and putting it in his pocket. "Thanks."

"Seriously, how long before we get to Woodstock? The Bone Man only gave us a few hours. We need to rescue Marilee." She drummed her fingers on the dash. "Can we make his time line?"

He shot her a sidelong glance, realizing he couldn't avoid telling her any longer. Fine. Sometimes the truth was hell. "You're not going to Woodstock."

She stared. "What do you mean? Of course I am. I have to."

"I'm going alone. I'm taking you to a *real* safe house this time."

"Alex—"

"Lyssa, you'd be a sitting duck. I won't allow that."

"Won't allow?" Her tight voice reverberated with anger. And worry.

Still, he had to make her see reason. "You have morning sickness. Despite everything, you might have more than yourself to think of here."

"More than myself." Her expression closed, making him almost regret saying the words. Almost. "You don't know that."

"No, and neither do you. Yet. Until we're certain, you've got to assume that you are pregnant."

Using logic to appeal to her, he knew she would listen. Lyssa might let emotion sway her, but in the short time he'd known her, she'd never disagreed with common sense.

"Just because I might be…"

He waited. She didn't complete the sentence. As though saying the words might make the pregnancy more real.

"Is it that difficult for you to swallow? The idea that you might be carrying my child?"

She turned her head, staring out the window instead of answering.

Her lack of response was answer enough. While it stung, he shouldn't have expected anything more. Not yet. Lyssa had still not fully adjusted to the concept of shape-shifters, never mind the idea she might be pregnant with one.

Instead of pressing, he swallowed back any further comments. They would deal with this issue later. For now, it would be enough if he could merely convince her to stay out of harm's way. "You need to think carefully. This is a serial killer we're talking about. He's insane. If you do as he asks, he's going to kill you."

"And if I don't, Marilee is dead."

"I'll get her out."

Turning her head, she stared at him. He saw no hope in her expression. Only the bleak certainty of loss.

Her next words confirmed it. "Don't make promises you can't keep."

A cold knot settled in his chest. "I don't."

"I want to go."

"If I have to worry about keeping you safe, I'll lose focus." Again, he spoke only truth. From the tight set of her jaw, he knew she didn't want to hear it. Tough. She'd asked for the truth. That didn't mean she had to like it.

Chapter 11

A small sign advertised a retail nursery a quarter mile away. When he saw the place on the right, packed full of weekend shoppers, he turned in and parked behind a black Tahoe that fleetingly reminded him of Carson's.

Lyssa tugged on her seat belt. "Why are we here?" She glanced around, her expression bleak. "This nursery? Reminds me of what I've lost."

He cursed. Stopping at a nursery might not have been a good idea. He hadn't thought of what it might mean to her when he'd pulled in. "This was the first place I saw. Nothing more. Come on, Lyssa. We need to talk. Decide on a plan."

"If you mean a plan that doesn't include me, you're wasting your time."

"Lyssa—"

With a half smile, half grimace, she shook her head.

"I'm going. End of discussion. I need your help, yes. We've got to get Marilee out."

He'd had enough. He'd tried caution, and warnings. She wanted to go, thought she could help? Time for a reality check.

"Fine. You want to go, go. But I need to know your qualifications."

"What do you mean?"

"List your special skills. Can you fight?"

"I told you, I took a self-defense class."

"Martial arts?"

"Some. I finished the class. I'm pretty good at it. But like I said, it's not enough."

He kept his face expressionless. "You've asked me to teach you to shoot? Do you have any previous weapons training? Have you ever handled a gun?"

She blinked. "No. But you're going to show me to use one."

"Do you even own a gun?"

"No." She bit her lip.

"A knife?"

An even longer hesitation this time. "Well, no."

He continued, even though he felt like he was beating her with his brutal words. Still, better this now than her facing harsh reality at the violent hands—and teeth—of the Bone Man.

"Okay, so you know a bit of self-defense." He kept his tone brisk, professional. One colleague to another. "You don't have a gun or a knife, nor do you know how to use either. Even if I teach you to shoot, it takes months, sometimes years, to become a skilled marksman. So you won't have that. You plan to charge in and…do what?"

Looking him straight in the eye, this time she didn't hesitate at all. "I don't know. You've got to help me, Alex. I might not become a skilled sharpshooter, but if you show me how, I can aim and fire. If I shoot him with a silver bullet, he'll die, right?"

While part of him admired her daring nature, stupid heroics wouldn't keep anyone alive. "Most people don't have what it takes to kill a man in cold blood. Can you honestly say you can point a gun at his chest, dead on, and kill him? Can you?"

She looked away.

"No lies, Lyssa." He threw her own words back at her.

Finally, she shook her head. "I don't know."

"You can't. He'll kill you." Flat, unemotional. If he needed to hammer her with the truth she claimed to love, so be it.

"Maybe I can't." Glaring at him, her eyes burned. "But you can. You can be my backup, my bodyguard. Either way, I have no choice. I've got to be there. I can't let Marilee die. He'll kill her if I don't show up."

"There's got to be another way."

She shook her head. "If there is, I don't see it."

"A decoy." Though grasping at straws, Alex liked the idea. "Another woman—a trained FBI agent or cop who looks like you. We'll put her in your clothes so she has your scent."

Before he'd even finished, she'd lifted her chin in that stubborn way of hers. "No way. Once the Bone Man finds out he's been duped, he'll be furious. Marilee won't stand a chance."

"We'll take him out long before he realizes."

"I can't risk Marilee's life."

"Her life? What if he lied? Serial killers, mass murderers, hell—all criminals have been known to do that. What if Marilee's already dead?"

Shock ripped across her face. "No. She couldn't be. He couldn't, wouldn't have—"

"Wouldn't he? Did you hear her voice?"

"You know I didn't."

"Then you don't really know. You could be risking yourself for nothing. Not just yourself—what if you are pregnant? What about the baby? Lyssa, we haven't been to a doctor."

"Well, we can't find one along the way now, can we? We don't have time. Marilee's my best friend. I'm not going to take the chance of being too late. You don't know if she's dead or alive. You don't know for sure."

The more he thought about it, the more he liked the idea of a decoy. As long as he was involved, he could make sure she even smelled like Lyssa, which was how the Bone Man would identify her.

"Let's try using a decoy. I'll go along, stay hidden. That way I can take the Bone Man out without worrying about your safety."

She still looked doubtful, but he could tell she was considering it. "What about Marilee?"

"The decoy will be a trained professional. She'll get your friend out." He didn't tell her that percentage-wise, Marilee was most likely already dead. "I need to talk to Trask." Avoiding looking at her, afraid his thoughts might show on his face, he punched in the number. After two rings, voice mail picked up. Odd. Rather than leaving a message, Alex ended the call.

Watching him with the look of a hostile witness, Lyssa crossed her arms. "Well?"

"No answer. I'll try him again in a few minutes."

"Good. I want to know how this happened." Eyes blazing, she glared at Alex. "Ask Trask that for me, will you? Find out why he wasn't able to protect Marilee."

He jerked his head in a quick nod. "That's what I'd like to know. They should have been watching for him. Especially since the guy managed to get past them twice. Even the profiler said he thought the Bone Man was still in the area. After he torched your house and shop, you'd think they'd have beefed up the patrols."

She sighed. "Alex, I'm worried. About Marilee, about this poor, unknown woman you want to send in my place. I still don't know…it's not her battle, it's mine."

"She'll be trained in law enforcement. FBI or state police. She'll be willing to take the risk—it's our job. We can't afford to back away from danger. Not if we want to stop the criminals."

Lyssa stared hard at him. "I hadn't thought of it like that. I'm angry, too, as well as afraid. Furious with Trask and the cops who promised to protect me. If I'd believed them and stayed there, I'd be dead now. I've lost my house, my business, because they let the Bone Man in."

She took a deep breath. "But that's not important. I can rebuild, restock. Losing possessions is nothing compared to what they've allowed him to do now. He's got my best friend in the whole world. We've got to make sure your plan with this decoy works. We've got to save Marilee."

"We'll get the bastard." And they would, as long as he kept his focus. This he swore. And if Marilee was alive, he'd get her out. No way in hell he wanted to lose another innocent to evil.

"God, I hope she's all right. She must be terrified, especially if she's seen him change into a wolf."

"Most likely he hasn't shown himself to her." Alex didn't add what he thought—once the Bone Man let Marilee see him change, she was dead. He killed only as his wolf self. "If he calls you again, ask him to let you speak with her."

Her eyes went round. "Calls me again? Crap." Holding up her cell phone, she turned it around in her hand, examining the gray plastic as though she thought it might bite her. "Do you really think—?"

"Yes. Definitely. He'll call again."

Another swallow, another movement of her graceful throat. He thought fleetingly of how badly he wanted to kiss the hollow there, at the base of it, then forced his attention back to things that truly mattered.

Like keeping her alive. Focus.

He shot her a glance, pulling his own cell phone from the belt clip. "I'm going to try Trask again, I really need to talk to him. I want to run this decoy idea past him. He can find her—someone in the FBI who looks enough like you to fool the Bone Man."

"What about scent? You said he'd be able to smell me."

"She can wear your clothes. Your perfume." He gave her a hard look. "It's worth a shot. I don't want you risking yourself if we can find another way."

Dividing his attention between Lyssa and his cell phone, Alex waited for the FBI agent to pick up.

Five rings. Six. Then voice mail. Again.

"That's odd." He tried the call once more.

Still no answer.

Damn. He clenched his teeth. "Something's wrong."

She looked at him, inhaling sharply when she caught sight of his expression. "A feeling?"

"Yeah."

"What is it?"

"I don't know." Then, taking a deep breath, he willed himself calm. "Most likely he's in the middle of a meeting. I should have left a message."

Her gaze never left his face. "He has caller ID. Your call will show up. Surely he'll call you back."

"Yeah." Putting the car in reverse, he glanced over his shoulder and pulled out onto the road. "In the meantime, there's one other thing we need to do." He signaled, taking the next exit.

In a few minutes they left that road and turned twice. They now traveled on a deserted back road, surrounded by rolling green fields and shadow-shrouded forests.

"I'm glad I'm not driving." Lyssa frowned. "I'm lost. Where are we going?"

"Just a minute." He flashed what he hoped was a reassuring smile. Turning yet again, this time onto a gravel road, he slowed, then pulled off onto the shoulder. Unlocking his glove box, he removed a cloth-wrapped bundle.

"Shooting practice." Unwrapping the parcel, he handed the weapon to her, butt first. "This was my grandmother's revolver—Smith & Wesson, model thirty-six. She used to carry it in her purse. My grandfather gave it to my sister when she passed away. Brenna doesn't like guns, so I ended up with it. The grip is perfect for a woman's hand."

"Your grandmother's revolver?"

"She liked to shoot. She was a pretty good marksman too. Here, take it. It's time we taught you how to use a gun."

Accepting the black pistol gingerly, she lifted a brow.

"Does this mean you've changed your mind about the decoy?"

He couldn't help it, he laughed. "Hell, no." She'd looked so savage, so intent, like she planned to track and kill the Bone Man as soon as she was confident of her shooting skill. "I want you to be able to defend yourself, just in case."

"Do you have silver bullets?" From the way she asked, she expected him to say no.

"Yes." He held up a box. "Right here. But we won't use them for practice. They're too hard to come by."

"What's a shape-shifter doing with silver bullets?"

"The council gave them to me. They knew I'd need them."

This surprised her. Closing her mouth, she lifted the gun. "I like the handle."

He grinned. "They're custom-made walnut grips. Grandpa got them for my grandmother. And this revolver takes five bullets instead of the customary six, so it's unusual."

"You sound like you really like this gun." She turned the pistol over in her hand, examining it. "It's pretty, as far as guns go."

"They quit making this particular model a few years ago, but it's always been one of my favorites. It's small and easy to carry, but still packs a punch."

"What do you mean?"

"It's a .38 caliber. Plenty of power behind the shells."

"This feels surprisingly heavy." Turning it to study it, she again flashed him that savage smile. "I like the way it looks. Small, but efficient. Deadly." Her smile widened.

"Bloodthirsty little thing, aren't you?"

At his words her smile vanished. "The Bone Man's got Marilee. I want him dead."

"Me, too." He wanted to kiss her. He touched her arm instead.

"I've no experience with guns." She moved away. "As a matter of fact, I've always been afraid of them."

"If you weren't, I'd worry about your sanity." With his hand over her wrist, he showed her how to push the load-release button with her right thumb and then flip the cylinder out.

"This is not an automatic," he explained. "You can't point and shoot, over and over. Each time, you have to cock the hammer manually. Automatics are quicker, but they also leave the shells behind to be used as evidence."

"That sounds like a criminal's logic."

"Maybe." He shrugged. "But law-enforcement officers have to be careful, too, especially when we're undercover." Opening another long velvet-wrapped box, he removed four bullets and assisted her with the loading process.

"This doesn't have a safety, so we won't put one in the chamber yet. It'll go when you cock the hammer. Time for target practice."

The first few times she fired, he kept his hand over hers, his arm under. When he released her to shoot on her own, she had to hold the gun with two hands. Her aim improved with each shot. The paper targets that he'd made were ripped to shreds.

"Good job." Handing her a box of shells, he flashed a smile, taking her breath away.

She inhaled, trying to look nonchalant. "I'm pretending each is a part of the Bone Man's body." What she didn't say was that doing so brought her a savage, primitive sort of pleasure.

"Good. If you ever come face-to-face with him, aim for the chest or the head. One shot won't kill him. Two might."

The thought of coming face-to-face with her hated enemy made her shiver.

"We'd better go." She went to hand him back the gun, but he waved her off.

"Not yet. Shoot one more round. I want to make sure you can handle yourself. Reload. Then I want you to keep it. It's small enough for you to carry it in your purse."

Frowning, she nodded. As he'd taught her, she pressed the release button and pushed out the cylinder. Accepting the bullets from him, she loaded five, this time placing one directly in the chamber. Taking aim at the last remaining target, she squeezed the trigger and fired. Dead on. She repeated the process. Again. The paper shredded where the bullet hit. She took careful aim. Fired. Direct hit. One more shot, then the last. Finally the gun clicked.

"Empty." Alex reached inside the car. "Now for the silver ammo." Emerging once more, he tossed her a small box. "I want you to keep it loaded. Since there's no safety, only load four. You don't want to keep a bullet in the chamber while you're carrying. It might accidentally go off."

Mimicking her earlier movements, Lyssa opened the chamber and reloaded. When she clicked it closed, she looked up at him, striving to keep her face expressionless. "Done."

"Great. Wrap it back up and put it in your purse." He clapped her on the shoulder. "Let's get back on the road. The cell signal is weak out here. We need to get closer to civilization so I can try Trask again."

It took only a moment for her to do as he'd asked. Surprisingly, the small pistol nestled in her bag like it belonged there.

Alex felt none of the relief he'd expected to feel knowing Lyssa was armed. She was proficient with the weapon, true, but he'd seen trained DEA agents freeze in the face of danger. He could only hope she never had to face the true test. If he could get to the Bone Man quickly, she wouldn't have to.

Once they reached the main road, Alex flipped open his phone and hit Redial. This time, he got an answer.

"Hello." The slightly accented voice wasn't Trask.

"Who the hell are you?"

Silence. Then "Who is this?"

Alex heard caution and a threat in the controlled voice. "DEA. Alex Lupe. And you are?"

The other man's exhalation carried across the lines. "Special Agent Johnson, FBI. I'm acting SAC."

"What? Where's Trask? I've got an emergency."

Again the silence. Tension so thick it felt solid coiled from the phone to Alex's gut. "Where the hell is Trask? Put him on the phone. Now."

Silence, then he heard the faint sound of Johnson handing the phone to someone else.

"Lupe? Is that you?" Another voice, rough with pain. Trask.

"What the hell happened? You sound like you've been run over by a truck."

The special agent chuckled, a painfully dry sound that ended in a hacking cough. "In a way I have. I met the Bone Man's pet."

Alex stilled.

"I was right—it wasn't a dog." Trask coughed again.

"It was a freakin' huge wolf. Wild. Probably rabid. It was foaming at the mouth. The doctors are making me start the series of shots."

"Rabid?" Rabies caused insanity. There had been only a few documented cases of shifters becoming infected while in their wolf self, usually by eating a rabid squirrel or rabbit. If the Bone Man had contracted the disease, this would explain the King Nebeshed delusions.

"Yeah." Trask cleared his throat. He was slurring his words. "Damn pain pills. Anyway, it was one hell of a way to go down. Damn thing tore me up."

"A wolf." He forced himself to sound surprised.

"Yeah. I got the teeth marks to prove it. The thing nearly had me. But the Bone Man never showed himself."

Alex glanced once more at Lyssa. "We heard from him." Quickly, he told the FBI agent about Lyssa's call.

"Marilee?" Despite the pain rasping in his voice, and his obvious drug-induced confusion, Trask tried to attend to business. "Last time I saw her was right before it attacked me. Poking through the rubble of the nursery and Lyssa's house." He mumbled something unintelligible, then, "So he was after her when he got me. I was in the...the way." He coughed again, a painful sound.

Alex waited until the sound subsided. Quickly he outlined his plan, hoping Trask would understand him. The man sounded out of it. "Can you help me?"

"I can't get you the decoy. Get Johnson to help."

"I'll let you know. I need some information from you. I've got to take Lyssa to another safe house."

"What's wrong with the first one?"

Alex glanced at Lyssa. Though she didn't like him to lie, no way was he informing Trask of his earlier deception. "It might have been compromised."

Trask swore. "Is there a mole?"

"Inside?" Alex looked at Lyssa again. She watched him intently. "It's possible. Is there a way you can get me a location on a secured line?"

"Can't, not here."

Damn. "Is there someone you trust who can do it?"

A pause. Alex could imagine Trask trying to think.

"Never mind. Asking anyone would be way too dangerous for Lyssa. The FBI has...offices...near Wicket Hollow. Take her there. It's secure."

"Thanks." Alex let the other man hear his gratitude. "Tell me how to get there."

Trask did, mumbling and slurring. Then, after another round of hacking shook him, he swore. "Johnson is good, but he's green. And the Staties are here?"

Great. Knowing them, they'd leak to the press. Especially if they found out about Marilee's kidnapping. That's all they needed, to have TV news blow the decoy's cover. "So we keep this under wraps."

"Yeah. You know how that goes."

Alex did. Everybody jockeying for superior bragging rights. "Trask, the feds are in charge here and it's gonna stay that way."

"Damn straight. This is my case, my investigation." He coughed again, then cursed. "I want out of this damn hospital."

"Take it easy." Alex could understand. Trask's dogged dedication to his cases was legendary. "Let them fix you up first. Then you can get back on the job."

"They say after the surgery, it'll be touch and go. If

I live, hell, I know they won't let me out of the hospital for a couple weeks at least."

"If you live?" Alex froze. "Trask, what the hell happened to you?"

"I'm under heavy guard."

Not an answer. "Answer me. How bad?"

"Look, I can't talk. They'll be wheeling me into surgery in a minute."

"Surgery for what?"

Trask mumbled something unintelligible, though Alex caught the word *reattach*. Now it was his turn to swear.

"Tell Johnson to arrange for the decoy. We're on our way. We'll be there in an hour." With a savage motion, he flipped the phone closed.

"What happened?" Lyssa sounded calm, though her eyes blazed and he could see the rapid pulse fluttering in her throat. Once he filled her in, she slammed her fist against the dashboard. "Trask was trying to protect her?"

"Yeah." Matching anger channeled into a strong urge to change. He fought it. "Trask's only human. No match for the Bone Man's strength." He didn't mention teeth and claws.

She took a deep breath and swallowed, all the while keeping her determined gaze fixed on him. "Maybe you *are* too close to the situation."

"No, I'm not." He tightened his hands on the steering wheel. "I'm the only law officer involved who truly understands what we're up against."

"Call in some others."

He stared at her. "What?"

"Pack guys. You said your kind are all over the place.

There must be more than a few in law enforcement you can enlist for help."

He thought about that for a moment. He knew several Pack members who'd be happy to help. Hell, Reed Hunter, Leaning Tree's Sheriff, had even volunteered at the council meeting. But Alex told Lyssa the same thing he'd told Reed. "I would bring in more of my own people if I could, but it's the fed's case, their ballgame. Trask only allowed me to get involved on the strength of an old favor. And now he's out of the game. No Lyssa, I'm going to have to go up against the Bone Man alone, since I alone know what he is."

She took a deep breath, pinching the top of her nose between her thumb and forefinger. "A werewolf."

He bit back the automatic rebuttal that sprang to his lips. In this case, the hated term actually applied. "Right. A werewolf."

"I know you told me silver bullets and fire would kill him, but should we get some garlic and a wooden stake too?"

Despite himself, he had to laugh. "Wrong monster. That only works on vampires."

"Vampires." She swallowed. He could see she wanted to ask if they were real. The question hovered there, in the impossible green of her eyes. He was relieved when she didn't. After all, she'd asked for truth. He hated to be the one to destroy every last illusion she might have.

Lyssa brushed her hair away from her face. "What next?"

"We're going to the FBI office near Wicket Hollow. Trask is sending an Agent Johnson to meet us there. He should have the decoy with him. She'll need to study you and will have to borrow some of your clothing, preferably worn so it has your scent. Once she's ready, we'll send her in. I'm going to insist I be allowed to back her up."

"You really think this will work?" She sounded doubtful.

"It's got to work."

"But if it doesn't? What if it only pisses him off?"

"Then—" reluctance colored his voice "—he could go on a total rampage, determined to bring down anyone who gets in his way."

"He'll kill Marilee, won't he?" Though she spoke quietly, he could hear her underlying horror. "If this doesn't work, he'll kill her and it will be all our fault."

Like it had been when Carson had lost his entire family. Alex had known about the hit, tried to stop it, but arrived too late to save them. Carson's wife and five-year-old daughter had died. Carson had blamed Alex for their deaths for a long time after, until he'd met Brenna and learned the truth. Alex couldn't entirely fault him either—his own guilt had consumed him, becoming the driving force behind the taking down of the drug-dealing gang Hades Claws.

Alex couldn't speak for a moment, so blinding was his rage and sorrow. When he finally could force words from his throat, he kept his voice steady only by a fierce act of will. "If he wants to kill Marilee, I don't think there's a hell of a lot we can do to stop him. All I know is we've got to try."

She didn't respond.

Alex pressed the accelerator harder. The growl of the motor was the only sound as the car ate up the miles.

"Lyssa, until he's caught, I want you to watch your back."

She made a strangled sound. "I will. But if we fail and he goes on a rampage, how will you stop him?"

She wanted honesty—he'd give her honesty. "I don't know. But I will. I have to."

"Is there any way you can make me into a shifter?"

"What?" Her question so shocked him, he nearly lost his focus on controlling the car.

"One of you." She narrowed her eyes. "If I was like you and could become a wolf, then I could go in after him. Once he thought he had me, I could change. I'd be stronger, more savage. I could take him down."

He wanted to kiss her. "Shifters are born, not made." Keeping his tone gentle, he tried to let her down easily.

"You can't just bite me or something?"

"No. All those legends are false. Biting you won't do anything to you but hurt you. It's not a disease you can catch. We're shifters because of an extra gene that affects our blood."

"Oh." She sounded disappointed. "I wanted a piece of him, too. Well then, can't you find another shifter to act as decoy?" She wondered why she hadn't thought of this before. "Wouldn't one of your own kind be better equipped to deal with him?"

Alex looked grim. "Yes, but we always recognize our own. The Bone Man would know as soon as he got close enough that she wasn't you."

"You said that before, but you weren't specific. How?"

"Aura. Energy. I'm not sure what to call it. But I can recognize another Pack member immediately. It's the same with all of us. Like recognizes like." He glanced at his watch. "Speaking of the Pack, the council will be expecting a report tonight, too."

"The council." She sounded surprised, as if she'd forgotten about them. "They're worried, aren't they?"

"Of course. If he goes on a rampage, mere humans won't stand a chance against him. Too many innocents will end up dead. That's why I've got to stop him before it gets worse."

With Alex driving his sports car like it was meant to be driven, they reached Wicket Hollow in less than an hour. The sky had darkened, threatening rain. The overcast sky mirrored the expression on Lyssa's face.

Lyssa. Brave, sweet Lyssa, with her fierceness and gumption. He shook his head. She'd actually wanted to become a shifter so she could rush in and defend her best friend against the evil enemy. She had no real idea of the kind of menace they actually faced and, if he could, he'd like to keep it that way. The worst human serial killer times ten didn't equal the Bone Man. If they weren't careful, there'd be a bloodbath.

Chapter 12

Once Alex fell silent, Lyssa felt absurdly grateful—and guilty, too. Though she couldn't imagine herself as a werewolf, it had been worth a shot.

That left them with the decoy. Even if she still wasn't entirely sure about this plan, for Marilee's sake, she would pray it worked.

Alex's cell phone rang. He looked at her before reaching for it. "Trask said he'd have Johnson call me."

Lyssa kept her gaze locked on his while he answered.

"We just drove past Esoppus—we're almost there. Five minutes, tops." Alex clicked the phone closed. "Johnson found someone. They're already there."

Someone. In a few minutes the decoy would no longer be a faceless, nameless woman willing to risk her life for someone she didn't even know. If she hadn't appreciated the risks law-enforcement people took before now, Lyssa gained an entirely new appreciation for them.

"I won't let anything happen to her." Alex touched her shoulder. "Don't worry."

Like he'd read her mind. "What if they won't let you go?"

"I'm going with her, Lyssa. No way in hell I'm letting the decoy do this without me."

Alex. The thought of anything happening to him... Unbearable. She couldn't even think it. So instead she focused her attention on what lay immediately ahead—training the decoy to act and look as much like her as possible.

When they pulled up to a fifties-era, russet-colored brick building, Alex killed the motor and turned to look at her.

"Ready?"

Heart in her throat, she nodded.

He pushed open his door and got out. Remembering his earlier warning to watch her back, Lyssa waited until he'd crossed around the rear of the car before climbing out herself.

A brusque nod told her he approved.

At the door, Alex pushed a button and spoke to someone she couldn't see behind dark glass. A buzzer sounded and Alex pulled open the door.

Once inside, a stone-faced guard with black hair in a buzz cut directed them to a conference room. Like a lot of what she'd seen on TV and in the movies, this room was painted puke-beige, the better to make it look austere and sterile.

Alex dropped into a metal chair and, leaning back, crossed his legs at the ankles. Too nervous to sit, Lyssa paced, wondering how he could appear so relaxed.

A moment later, a tall black man entered the room. Following behind him were two women and another man.

Unfolding his frame from the chair, Alex stood.

Handshakes were made all around, though no one volunteered their names. It appeared they'd have a choice of decoys, as both of the women were slender blondes with similar height and bone structure as Lyssa. They wore identical black windbreakers with FBI emblazoned across the back in yellow, and matching black T-shirts.

The only one dressed in a navy suit and tie, the tall man stepped forward. "I'm Johnson." He asked Lyssa to stand between the other two women. They were then told to turn, left to right, then back again, moving in unison, like a choreographed line of halfhearted dancers.

Johnson looked at Alex. Grim-faced, Alex walked past them, pausing in front of each woman as though deep in thought. His nostrils flared, telling Lyssa he was checking out their scents to see if any came close to hers.

So would the Bone Man. She shivered. Better safe than sorry.

In the end, Alex chose the woman on Lyssa's left, name still unknown. Lyssa dug in her bag and handed her one of her old T-shirts and a pair of jeans. The woman took them, nodded once and turned to go. But then she hesitated, looking back over her shoulder, her gaze meeting Lyssa's. Lyssa could have sworn she saw fear in the other woman's eyes. But before she could comment, or even check again, the female FBI agent spun on her heel and left the room.

Johnson touched Lyssa's shoulder, his expression

not even changing when she jumped. "We need to take some pictures."

Dutifully she stood still, presenting her left profile, then her right. She felt as though they were making mug shots. When he'd finished snapping the photos, the FBI agent gave her a grim nod before he too exited.

"Time to go." Alex took her hand. "You're cold."

"I don't like this."

The look he gave her told her he didn't either. "I know. I've got to go brief her and work out the plan. Do you want to wait here or in the cafeteria?"

Though the thought of food made her stomach turn, the idea of staying in this austere, freezing room seemed worse. "The cafeteria. Maybe I can get a ginger ale or something."

As soon as she'd finished speaking, yet another man in a suit entered the room. "Follow me, please."

Lyssa looked at Alex. He nodded, so she did.

Their footsteps echoed as they walked what seemed to be a labyrinth of identical hallways. Her escort didn't speak, negotiating the many twists and turns with a military precision.

Finally, she could stand it no longer. "Is this usual?"

He looked at her. Not smiling, not answering either.

"Is it usual?" she pressed, determined to make him talk. "The way you're getting that woman ready to be my decoy?"

"No ma'am." Wooden-faced, he pushed open a door at the end of one hall. "Here you are."

When she walked past him into the deserted cafeteria, she saw two vending machines against the far wall. Turning to thank her escort, she realized he'd already left.

A chocolate bar and a cola were not the healthiest choice for a snack, but Lyssa didn't care. Hungry and groggy and out of sorts, she needed something and a quick caffeine fix might help. About to punch the button for the soft drink, she thought of an article she'd read warning pregnant women against too much caffeine. Better safe than sorry. She got a lemon-lime beverage and a granola bar instead, and settled down in one of the uncomfortable plastic chairs.

Eating slowly, she finished her snack and sipped her soda. A large, industrial wall clock ticked off the minutes. Ten, then twenty minutes passed.

Still no Alex. Surely he wouldn't go to meet the Bone Man without telling her. Would he? Then again, he'd left after Claire's funeral without even a lame explanation. She'd simply woken up to an empty bed and realized his duffel bag was gone.

She sat for as long as she could stand it, then stood and began to pace, telling herself the exercise would help work off the sugar calories she'd just consumed.

Half an hour. No Alex. Back and forth, her passing reflection in the glass wall looking more frazzled with each round of the clock's second hand.

Forty-five minutes. Still no Alex. Fine. She'd give him a hour. Then, FBI protocol be damned, she was going looking for him.

Exactly fifty-nine minutes later, the same man who'd escorted her earlier appeared in the doorway. When he stood at attention, she half expected him to salute her.

"Ma'am? I'm here to take you back to Agent Johnson's office."

"Will Alex be there?" Lyssa pushed her hair back from her face, wishing she didn't feel so weak and shaky.

"Follow me."

Since he turned and strode away an instant after he spoke, Lyssa had to hurry to catch up, which infuriated her. Still, she had no choice. If staying in the empty cafeteria wasn't her idea of hell, wandering the endless, featureless hallways with their beige walls and equally colorless floors would come close.

"Take me to Lyssa." Furious, Alex pushed himself to his feet, glaring at Agent Johnson. "Damn you, I told you I *had* to go with the decoy." He swore again. "Hell, you didn't even have the woman spend any time with Lyssa. Now you're telling me she didn't wear Lyssa's clothes?" He swore again. "You have no idea how important that was. I can't believe you sent her in with no more preparation than this."

Johnson looked unimpressed. "She didn't need any more preparation. She's a trained agent. This will be a simple operation."

Hellhounds. "Simple?" Alex couldn't believe it. "You have no idea what we're dealing with."

The other man gave him a grim smile. "Ah, but we do. We're FBI—we deal with psychos like this all the time. He's a serial killer. We deal with those more than we'd like." He held up a hand when Alex seemed about to speak. "Yes, we know he's insane. Most of them are. We've done this before, Lupe."

"I don't doubt that." Alex took a deep breath, trying to push back the rage, trying like hell to will himself calm. He should have gone as backup. The Bone Man was his. *His.* "Tell me your plan."

"Agent Womack goes in, presents herself to the Bone Man as a trade for his hostage. When he goes for her, she takes him down." He snapped his fingers. "Easy as that."

They had no idea. Damn.

"Easy?" Alex echoed. "How long have you been with the bureau, Agent Johnson?"

The other man's smile faded. "Long enough. Why?"

"Have you ever dealt with an operation that went exactly as planned?"

"I—"

"Have you?" Alex roared.

"This one will." But Johnson's confidence now sounded forced. He glanced at his watch. "Agent Womack will be making contact soon."

"Alone. Totally unprepared. A lone woman with a madman. Is that standard operating procedure?"

"We've got a team backing her up."

"But she still went in alone."

"They can get to her if anything goes wrong."

Alex shook his head. "You're certain of that?"

"You know as well as I do when we've got a perp this crazy, all bets are off."

"Exactly! That's why I can't understand why you didn't let me go. You put that woman's life at risk."

Stone-faced, the agent in charge glared back. "It's a risk she's willing to take. We're all willing to take it, if we can get that idiot off the streets."

"You fool!" Alex snarled, battling back the sharp, sudden urge to change. The wolf part of him fought to surface, snarling. He forced it back. He could go longer than this and had, when he'd been undercover, but extreme emotion intensified his need. "Again, you don't know what you're dealing with here."

"And you do?"

"Yes. That's why I asked to go with her."

Johnson shrugged. "We declined your request. You're not even FBI. There are no drugs involved here. No gun smuggling. DEA has no reason to get involved."

"No reason? Hellhounds, this guy is after my wife."

"We'll take care of it." Johnson stood. Jamming his hands in his pockets, he gave an impersonal smile. "I think this interview is finished."

"Great." Alex had nothing else to say. There was no point. He'd worked for the federal government too long. "Where's Lyssa? I need to let her know what's going on."

Johnson consulted the clock. "We sent a man to get her. She should be here any minute."

"Will they let you know when the decoy's made contact?" Knowing she was as good as dead made it impossible for Alex to use the woman's name.

"Yes. They'll call me. Oh, and Lupe? We won't be able to let you or your wife leave yet."

"What?" Alex turned slowly. "What the hell are you talking about?"

"You can't go anywhere until this thing is over." Expression unapologetic, Johnson shrugged. "We can't risk either of you blowing Womack's cover."

"Right." While this made sense, Alex knew the real reason they didn't want him out on the street. They were afraid he'd go charging in and mess up their pristine operation.

With a brief dip of his chin, Johnson let him know he'd interpreted correctly. "Once contact has been made, we don't estimate this will take much more than an hour. My team will be in constant communication with me."

"If they're not going in with her, how will they know?"

"She's wired." Johnson sounded confident. "We'll hear everything the perp has to say."

And worse. Cursing under his breath, Alex resumed listening for Lyssa's footsteps. He prayed their rushed operation wouldn't be the mistake he feared it was.

Closing his eyes, he concentrated on breathing. He wanted to present a calm facade for Lyssa.

Lyssa.

He heard her before he saw or scented her. The light tapping of her feet on the floor echoed ahead of her. When she rounded the corner and saw him, her eyes widened, then narrowed.

"I thought you'd gone." Crossing her arms, she ignored both her escort and Johnson. "Or is that why I'm here now, so you can tell me goodbye?"

Though she'd spoken harshly, Alex caught the fine tremor in her voice. Again he felt fury rise in him, unsuccessful this time in hiding it.

Her eyes widened. "What's happened?" she whispered.

"The decoy's gone."

"Gone? Without you?"

"Yeah. They sent her in alone. Without studying you, without your clothes, without me."

"What?" She looked from him to Johnson. "Are you serious?"

Alex answered for him. "Dead serious."

"Oh God."

"Come on you two." Falsely hearty, Johnson came up behind Alex and clapped him on the shoulder. "You're acting like you think this guy has some sort of superhuman powers or something."

"That's because he does." Speaking through clenched teeth, Alex shrugged off the other man's hand. "Don't touch me again."

The growl in his voice must have convinced Johnson, who took a quick step back. Alex felt his wolf-self rise, again fighting for release. Ruthless, he subjugated it.

Lyssa watched him, her expression horrified. "Tell me she'll be all right," she whispered. "Please."

"She'll be fine," Johnson interjected. "Give me a break. She's a trained professional. She can handle this guy."

"What kind of briefing did you give her?" Alex demanded.

"Standard."

Which could mean anything. Either way, it wouldn't be enough.

"What now?" Though Lyssa addressed Alex, her glance slid from him to Johnson and back.

"We wait."

Alex shook his head, keeping his frustrated rage under control. "Who's monitoring the transmissions? I want to listen."

"You can't—they're in a van behind her. But they're recording, so if you still feel the need later, we might let you hear it then."

"Can't you patch us in?"

Johnson raised his brows, as if such a request was unheard of. But Alex knew better—he'd done the same type of work himself, too many times to count.

"I don't think she needs to hear this." Indicating Lyssa, Johnson declined.

Alex caught himself about to bare his teeth. Instead, he shook his head, concentrating on slowing his heart rate.

As though she understood, Lyssa came over and slipped her arm around his waist. Instantly, stillness stole over him, the icy kind of calm under which he worked best, with every sense heightened.

He wanted to kiss her. He settled for squeezing her in a quick hug instead. She looked up, flashing him a smile. This time he couldn't resist touching her mouth lightly with his own.

Johnson cleared his throat. His phone rang—landline, less easily traced. He answered, spoke a few words, and replaced the receiver.

"Womack's at the meeting place, awaiting contact," he said. "Don't worry about her. Our team's in place."

"Where?"

"Hidden. In the woods near the rendezvous."

"How many men?"

Johnson ruffled some papers on his desk. "Seven."

"Not nearly enough. SWAT?"

"Same difference. They're surrounding the area. They'll close in at the first sign of trouble."

"No!" Lyssa stepped forward, her hands fisted at her sides. "What if he sees them? He said I had to come alone. Marilee's life is at stake here. He'll know if you have too many men in the woods."

Johnson gave her a hard look. "He won't know. We know what we're doing. No one is at risk, at least if we can help it. If your friend is still alive, we'll get her out."

"Of course she's still alive. I swear to you, if one single hair on her head is harmed—"

This time Alex provided the comfort. He reached out and brought her to him, drawing her back against his chest. She fell silent, the rise and fall of her chest showing her labored breathing. He could feel her pulse, fluttering like a captive dove against his arm.

Someone brought them coffee, steaming and hot. Alex accepted his gratefully. Lyssa declined, requesting water instead.

The phone on Johnson's desk rang again. He picked it up and listened. "She's made contact," he said, replacing the receiver.

"Now what?" Though Lyssa asked the question of Johnson, she looked up over her shoulder at Alex.

"Again, we wait."

Johnson seconded Alex's comment. "The team will notify us when they've got him." Confidence rang in his voice.

Alex could only hope the FBI agent was right. But none of these guys realized what kind of beast they were dealing with. And while Alex knew he had to keep it that way, he only hoped by doing so he didn't cause the loss of any more lives.

The desk phone rang a third time. Snatching it from the cradle, Johnson listened, his face going from impassive to horrified. Terse, he spoke a few words—monosyllables. When he replaced the receiver, he stared at Alex, his expression dazed.

"We got him but something went wrong. Agent Womack—the decoy—she's dead. There was a slaughter—a freakin' giant wolf or something. He took out most of our team. There are—" he swallowed "—bodies everywhere. We don't have a firm body count, but my agent said they're working on it. The hospital's been notified and emergency crews are en route."

Alex cursed. He took a step forward.

"Hold up." Johnson held up his hand. "We got him. He's dead—we took him down."

"The Bone Man? You know this for certain?" Alex wanted to grab Johnson by the throat, but settled for poking him in the chest instead.

The level of the other man's shock was so high, he didn't react. "Yes. He's dead. The agent who called me said they've IDed the body." Johnson wiped a shaky hand across his mouth. "We lost a lot of men. A hell of a lot of men. They were armed. He wasn't. His damn pet sure as hell wasn't."

"Pet?"

"Yeah. Damn thing got away."

"But the Bone Man's dead. You're sure of this?"

"Positive. Our men fired first. There was no return gunfire, yet we lost at least four men, five counting Womack. With no return gunfire. None. That doesn't make sense. I can't understand how it could happen."

"Agent Womack is dead?" Lyssa stepped forward, her face a study of fury and anguish.

"Yes." Johnson lowered his voice. "We lost her."

Lyssa stared at the other man, hard. Then she looked at Alex.

"I'm sorry," he told her.

"Not your fault." Lyssa inhaled, a sharp sound. "What about Marilee? Were you able to get her out?"

"No."

At the short answer, Lyssa reeled. Alex went to her, pulling her close to him while glaring at the other man, who now wouldn't meet his eyes.

"How…? When…?"

"My man didn't say. But with all due respect, ma'am." Johnson wouldn't even glance at them as he spoke, "Your friend was probably already dead long before we got there."

In his arms, Lyssa stiffened. She buried her face in his chest, her slender back shaking with the force of her sobs.

The sound of her weeping made Alex want to punch the wall.

Johnson's face contorted. He swore.

"You've got it all on tape, right?"

"We should. Like I said, she was wearing a wire."

"I'm going." Alex put enough force in his tone to let the other man know he would brook no argument. "Tell me how to get there."

Before Johnson could respond, his desk phone rang yet again. Answering, he spoke twice. Dropping the receiver back in the cradle, he gazed at Alex with shock stark in his eyes. "The men I have left are on their way here now."

"With the Bone Man's body?"

"No." Johnson peered at him like he'd lost his mind. "You know the drill. After the ME gets through, they'll take all the dead to the morgue. You can see the body there later."

Alex sighed, massaging the back of his neck. About to do the same, he saw Lyssa catch herself and grimace. She lowered her hand.

"There's really nothing you can do," she whispered.

In truth, he supposed there wasn't. If the Bone Man had changed at the moment of death, they'd think the large wolf was his dead pet. If not, it would be just a human body.

Still, he wanted to see the Bone Man's corpse with his own eyes. "How well have you protected the crime scene from possible contamination?"

"Don't even think about going out there, Lupe. I've sent in more men to guard it. They'll give out warnings, but anyone who tries to get past them will be shot."

"I'm worried about the media." Alex fixed a pleasant expression on his face. "But as long as you're sure it's secure… I'll stop by the morgue later."

"With her?" Johnson indicated Lyssa.

"Maybe. When can I hear the tape?

"They're bringing it now. Still, it'll be a couple of hours before you can listen."

"You're going over it first?"

"Of course." Johnson gave him a humorless smile.

Again, Alex had to forcibly restrain himself from grabbing the other man. "I'm a federal agent. You don't need to screen it before I hear it."

"You're not FBI. And then there's…" He indicated Lyssa with a dismissive wave.

"She doesn't need to hear it."

"I want to." Lyssa lifted her head, rubbing her eyes. Red and swollen from crying, nevertheless they burned with a rage—a feeling Alex could certainly relate to.

Still, in this instance he agreed with Johnson. She didn't need to hear the tape.

"Bad idea." Alex shook his head. "What good would it do, besides give you nightmares?"

"This is my problem, my fault. I should hear it."

"It's not your fault, understand me?"

"I still want to listen."

"You'll hear things you wish you hadn't."

Swallowing, she blinked. "I realize that."

"No, you don't." Cupping her chin, he turned her face up to his. Though his kept his expression bland for Johnson's sake, he hoped the connection they shared would allow her to understand him. "It will mark you, change you forever. Something so horrible…is impossible to forget. Believe me, I know."

"I have no choice. I've got to listen. This girl—Agent Womack—died in my place."

"He was a savage killer, ma'am." Agent Johnson, his expression closed, signaled to one of the other men, who disappeared out the door. "We have reasons for not letting civilians listen."

But Lyssa refused to be swayed. "I insist. I'll listen and I'll endure every horrific sound."

Finally, Alex understood. "You're doing penance."

"Maybe." Hollow-eyed, Lyssa glanced at him and nodded. "You're right. In a way, I am."

"Whatever," Johnson said. "Either way, we have to screen it. The team will be here in an hour or less. It'll be another couple hours before you can hear the tape."

Johnson seemed impatient with them, apparently eager to return to his duties as acting SAC.

"What about the team, the ones that are left? Can I talk to them?"

"Not yet."

"I want to hear what they have to say while everything's still fresh in their minds."

"You know better than that. Debriefing." Johnson sounded both glum and furious. "Five of our own have been lost. The team is in shock." He glanced once more at his watch. "The hospital is down the street. Stop in and check on Trask. I'll join you when debriefing's over. We'll come back together and listen to the tape."

Something in his tone…

"What exactly happened to Trask?" Hoping his soft

question would catch the man off guard, Alex focused on the other man's face.

"Trask?" Johnson lifted a brow. "I thought you'd talked to him."

"We did. He wouldn't tell me jack. When I asked him, he mumbled and hung up."

"I don't know how they kept him alive." Johnson bit out the words. "He lost a lot of blood when that thing ripped off his…" He swallowed, hard. "He could lose both of his legs."

Lyssa gasped. "Both his legs?"

"Yeah." Johnson looked at Alex. "They were bringing him into surgery when I left to meet you here. They might have to amputate—if he makes it."

Alex cursed.

Johnson's expression hardened. "Now it makes no difference to me whether you wait in the cafeteria or go and see Trask. I've got a couple of things I have to do. Then I plan to check on my boss before I come back and listen to the tape. Do whatever you want."

With those parting words, he stormed out of the room.

Chapter 13

They arrived at the hospital in less than five minutes. The building matched the overcast sky—gray and grim looking.

"That's one scary hospital." Lyssa knew her voice sounded remote. Shocked.

"Yeah." He parked the car, killed the engine, and looked at her as if unsure what to say. "I'm sorry about your friend."

"Marilee." Her throat closed up. Taking several deep breaths, it was a moment before she could speak. "Me, too."

"When all this is wrapped up, we need to talk."

She smiled softly, hiding her pain. "I know." Those were the exact words he'd used the night before he'd left her last time. As though he'd be there when she woke. With her radar out for lies, she'd known he hadn't been straight with her, but the end result was the same. He was gone. For whatever reason. This time she'd be better prepared. She would never again allow herself to drift into pretending they could have any kind of life together.

Obviously, Alex could. He put his arm around her and kept it there, all the way across the parking lot. He didn't release her until they reached the hospital's automatic doors. Together they crossed the polished floor to the front desk.

"We're looking for Walter Trask."

At first the receptionist couldn't locate him. She appeared confused as she scanned her computer screen. Finally, she looked up with a frustrated expression. "He's in surgery on the second floor. You can take the elevator up and wait in a small waiting room there."

"Thanks." Alex grunted, leading Lyssa where the receptionist pointed and punching the up button. They stepped inside, neither speaking. Lyssa didn't mind. If she tried to talk right now, she'd lose it.

When the elevator doors opened again, she instantly started forward. As she stepped out, the elevator seemed to move with her, making her stagger. "What the—?"

Instantly, Alex was at her side, his hand supporting her elbow. Though normally this would have irritated her, for some reason she actually needed his help to stand upright.

"Damn."

"What's wrong?" He leaned down close, his nose nearly touching hers.

"It's been a rough day. My nerves must be making me dizzy." She inhaled then exhaled, concentrating on her breathing. Slow and steady. Gradually, her vision cleared. She took another deep breath and willed her heart rate to slow. Finally, she lifted her chin. "I'm fine." To prove it, she took a step forward. Everything stayed in place.

"Good." Still holding her arm, they moved down the hallway.

"No nurses?" She pointed at the nurse's station, hating the way her hand shook. Nerves were a hassle. She kept telling herself the Bone Man was dead. It still felt like a lie.

"Maybe they're all busy."

They exchanged a look. But the odd prickly feeling at the back of her neck told her differently. She lifted a hand to rub there, freezing when she noticed Alex doing the exact same thing.

"Back of my neck itches." He glowered at her.

"Mine, too." They stared at each other. "But there's no danger here, right? The Bone Man's dead."

Finally, Alex shrugged. "Must be aftershocks. It's been a hell of a day."

They continued on, their footsteps absurdly loud in the still-deserted hallway.

"Some hospital."

He glanced at her. "This isn't normal. Something's wrong."

Something *was* off beam. She felt the wrongness of it creep over her skin like goose bumps.

Glancing at Alex, she saw in his face he felt it, too.

"Let's go find the surgery waiting area." She looked left to right. Still deserted. Decidedly un-hospital-like. "Why are we whispering?"

"I don't know." Again, the flash of a smile. "But I hope that waiting room has at least a couple of cops in it."

Together they followed the sign toward the surgical waiting area.

"Still not a single nurse."

"I know." They turned the corner and Alex cursed under his breath. The small waiting area was empty, the rows of blue vinyl and chrome chairs unoccupied by any warm bodies.

"No cops. Not even a federal agent." Alex shifted his arm—and hers—uneasily.

"Are we even on the right floor?"

"Yep. Second floor. This is the surgery waiting room the reception desk told us about."

"Maybe she was wrong."

"Can I help you?" Finally, a nurse. Balancing a metal tray laden with sample cups and a clipboard, she frowned at them.

"We're here for Walter Trask. He's in surgery."

"Who?"

"FBI agent. Trask. He's been hurt. Legs."

Her frown deepened. "And you are?"

Alex pulled out his ID and handed it to her. She studied it, alternating between the ID card and him. Then, seeming to make up her mind about something, she gave a curt nod.

"Wait here." With movements as abrupt as her speech, she pivoted and disappeared inside a room, taking Alex's ID with her.

"I don't like this." Lyssa took a deep breath.

"Me either." Moving so that their backs were against the wall, Alex scanned the area. "She must be undercover. FBI or police. She didn't seem like a nurse."

"I know. I got that, too. Must be that mystical *connection,*" she said, forcing a smile.

He didn't smile back.

A moment later the nurse returned and handed Alex back his ID. "You've been cleared. Follow me."

Without waiting to see if they would, she led the way down the hall, her rubber-soled feet making no sound on the linoleum floor.

Alex started after the nurse, leaving Lyssa to follow. Though she tried like hell to keep up, insistent nausea clogged her throat. Dratted flu again? Alex turned to wait for her and she waved him on. He shook his head, waiting for her to catch up.

When the nurse disappeared around a corner, Alex cursed under his breath. "Please wait."

An instant later the woman reappeared. "Problem?"

Her aggressive stance confirmed his suspicions. Put a shoulder harness on her and she looked ready to draw. "You're not a nurse, are you?"

"No." She glared at him before breaking into a reluctant smile. "FBI. Special Agent Matterling."

He held out his hand. "As you know from my badge, I'm Agent Lupe. This is my wife, Lyssa."

After the requisite handshake, Matterling seemed to soften somewhat. Squinting at Lyssa, she gave a jerk of her chin. "You look green around the gills. What's wrong with you?"

"I don't feel well." Lyssa managed to summon a wan smile, though even getting the words out required a major effort. "Flu or something."

The other woman nodded, though she didn't seem convinced.

Narrowing his eyes, Alex watched her closely.

"I'll be fine." She waved her hand. "Lead the way."

With Matterling in the lead, they turned another corner. Two uniformed officers guarded a door. They nodded at Matterling as she pushed through.

"Agent Trask is this way." She led them down yet another long hallway. "We've commandeered most of this floor. They're bringing the wounded here."

The wounded. From the messed up operation. Alex gave a nod of approval. "Now it makes sense. So what's up with the security precautions? We caught the guy who did this."

Shaking her head in disgust, Matterling pushed through another door. "I know. I would've liked to be in on it. But this is to keep the media out. They've been camped out like vultures in the emergency room." She shrugged. "Instead of bringing our people down there, they're shuffling them over here."

They turned yet another corner. A small crowd had assembled. Uniformed cops mingled with FBI agents in their trademark windbreakers. Lyssa estimated maybe twenty people were crowded in the small room. The air felt hot, cloying. She gagged as the ever-present nausea threatened again to erupt. She took several deep, heavy breaths, struggling to keep her equilibrium.

One of the men wearing khakis and a shirt and tie waved at Alex in recognition. Alex responded in kind.

"What's the status?"

"Trask is still in surgery. He lost a lot of blood, and they deemed his condition life-threatening."

"Any idea how much longer?"

The other man shook his head. "It's a complicated procedure. They'll finish when they finish. All we can do is wait until the doctor comes out and tells us he's done." After a hard glance at Lyssa, he returned to his position over by the window.

Lyssa staggered. She winced as the room kept moving after she'd stopped.

Alex started forward. "You're not okay, are you?"

She licked her lips and tried to speak, but couldn't. Instead, she mouthed the word *no*.

"You need to have a doctor look at you." Looking wildly around, he waved at a nurse. As she bustled over, he stopped her with a touch on her arm.

"We need a doctor."

The nurse looked from him to Lyssa and back again. "At the end of this hallway is a small examining room. Take her there and I'll bring a doctor." Pivoting around on her soft-soled shoes, she bustled away.

Alex lifted Lyssa's chin. "Can you make it down the hall?"

Forcing her eyes open, she swallowed. So far, so good. "Sure." She summoned a confidence she didn't really feel, especially since she had to close her eyes to keep the room from spinning.

"No problem." She tried to smile, but her feet seemed to tangle of their own accord. Struggling to keep from falling, her heart skipped as the edges of her vision grayed. All at once the ground tilted, rushing up to meet her.

When she next opened her eyes, she became aware that her surroundings had changed. They were in a room.

"I passed out again." Disgusted, she met Alex's eyes. "This is getting ridiculous."

"Yeah, well. The doctor's been here and left. She said she'd be back in a minute."

"Been here and left?" Lyssa goggled at him. "But it's only been a second, right?"

"No." Alex stood, jamming his hands into his pockets. The worry in his face scared her more than the thought of fainting did.

Lifting her head seemed to take an inordinate amount of energy. As she did, she noticed she wore a patterned hospital gown. Plucking at the fabric, she looked at Alex.

"The nurse and I got you undressed so the doctor could examine you." His face gave nothing away. "Your clothes are there." He indicated a neatly folded stack on a plastic chair.

"Fine." She sighed. "What did the doctor say?"

Alex looked away. "Nothing yet." She watched as he visibly summoned up a smile that did little to ease the harsh planes of his face.

"I'm all right though, aren't I?"

"Be glad I was able to catch you."

Not an answer. Still, she'd play along for now, until the doctor returned. "Why, did I hit something on the way down?"

The rough smile vanished. He cocked his head. "No."

She looked at her hands, her shirt. No blood. "Okay then, level with me. What's up? Why do you look so worried?"

As he glanced at her stomach, she had her answer. His next words confirmed it. "I hope the baby is all right."

"The baby?" Still, she too caught herself cradling one arm protectively across her abdomen. "How many times do I have to say it? I'm not pregnant. One negative test I could find fault with, but I did three. They were even different brands."

"How else can you explain this? You're sick in the

morning. You fainted." Serious, he studied her. "Is this normal for you? If you had the flu, there'd be other symptoms."

She started to shake her head, but decided not to bother dignifying his question with a direct answer. "It's got to be nerves. Or stress. A combination of the two. My life hasn't exactly been normal lately."

"We'll see." He looked away, as though expecting the doctor to show up any minute.

"What about Trask?" Changing the subject seemed the safest bet. She tried to sit up, but any sudden movements or even the attempt at one caused the world to tilt alarmingly again.

"He's not out yet. They promised to let me know." He glanced at the door, in the direction of the nurses' station. "I still haven't even seen any other nurses. Except for one or two, they must have pulled them all off this floor."

Bracing her elbows behind her, this time Lyssa succeeded in pushing herself up into at least a sitting position. "Upright's definitely better than prone."

"That depends." His wolfish smile came and went.

Because she felt her face heating, she focused instead on the strangely empty hall outside her room.

"Help me up."

"Let the doctor look at you first."

She bit her lip. "Are you sure she's coming back?"

"She said she would."

"How about if I wait here and you check on Trask?" Anything to keep him from staring at her like she was about to keel over any moment. "He's got to get out of surgery soon."

Immediately he shook his head. "No. We're waiting for the doctor to come back."

"I'm not an invalid," she groused. Grumbling under her breath, she succeeded in pushing herself up to a full sitting position.

The room stayed in one place.

Encouraged, she swung her legs over the side of the bed.

Shaking his head, Alex moved to help her. With his arm supporting her waist, she struggled to her feet. Again that uncomfortable sensation that her surroundings were moving while she stood still. Nausea filled her throat. Taking deep breaths, she concentrated on not getting sick.

Finally, everything settled back to the way it was supposed to be.

"Are you okay?"

Overly conscious of the welcome heat radiating from his body, yet glad of his arm supporting her, helping her, she nodded. "Give me a minute."

Ever since she'd been a child, she hadn't been able to stand anyone touching her when she felt ill. Though she didn't know why, Alex's touch didn't have the same effect.

So instead of pushing him away, she leaned into him and let his broad chest support her wobbly legs.

"Feeling better?" At the lighthearted voice, they both turned. A short, dark-haired woman in a white lab coat stood in the doorway. A younger woman, assistant most likely, bustled into the room carrying a tray of instruments.

"Do you want to stay or leave, sir?" The assistant asked. "Dr. Fallas needs to do an examination."

"I'm staying." Alex didn't budge.

The prospect of being examined by the doctor in

front of Alex sounded about as appealing as eating slugs. Lyssa's stomach turned.

"I'll be fine. Stand outside the door a minute or something." She tried to send him a message with her eyes, using the supposed connection he kept talking about.

Alex was having none of it. Folding his arms, he didn't move.

Lyssa felt her entire body flush. "Alex, if you don't leave, I'm not going to let them examine me. Then you won't know either way."

He stared at her, then jerked his head in what passed for a nod. Jaw set, he moved to the doorway and stood with his back to them.

"Can you close the door?"

"Lyssa—"

"Just leave it open a sliver, all right? I don't want to flash everyone who walks down the hall."

Finally he did as she asked, affording her a relative amount of privacy. Lyssa submitted to the examination, focusing herself on counting the water spots on the ceiling.

"All done." The doctor pulled of her gloves, smiling. "I'll need a urine sample and a blood sample."

Lyssa slid back, readjusting the hospital gown.

"Well?"

"What I saw did indicate a possible pregnancy. But we'll need to wait for the test results to be sure. It should only be a few minutes."

A possible pregnancy. Dimly conscious of the door opening, of Alex stepping inside, she managed a nod. Suddenly, she felt oddly weepy.

"You're not happy?" The doctor watched her closely.

"Happy?" Lyssa sniffed. "I'm not sure how I feel about this."

Alex came closer, reaching out to touch her cheek. He held up his finger. "You're crying."

"We'll be back in a minute," the doctor said. "Right now we'll leave you two alone to talk." She and her assistant left.

"Don't cry." Alex sounded helpless. "Please."

"I'm sorry." She wiped at her damp cheek. "I can't help it." The idea of a baby seemed overwhelming, period. The idea of a baby who might inherit the ability to change shape, to become a werewolf was...unthinkable.

"It's not that bad. You wouldn't be able to tell anything was different." Smoothing back her hair, Alex's voice was a deep, bass rumble. He seemed to instinctively read her thoughts.

"What do you mean?"

"Changeling babies are more like humans than not. And we've developed medications that keep them from changing until they're ready."

She raised her gaze to his face. His handsome, earnest, face. "Medications?"

"Yes." He shifted his weight from one leg to the other. "They're like allergy pills. They suppress the dormant gene and the desire to change."

For some reason this thought gave her comfort. If she was pregnant, her baby could be a normal, human infant. She wouldn't have to worry about coming in for a midnight feeding and finding a wolf pup in her child's crib.

A nurse poked her head into the room. "The doctor got called away to an emergency. If you want to wait in the waiting area, someone will come and get you."

Once dressed, Lyssa and Alex returned to the surgical waiting room. Crackers and water had settled her stomach and a shot of vitamins had given her strength. She actually felt human again, semi-strong, able to walk and talk and think.

A few minutes after they arrived, Trask's surgeon appeared, still in his operating-room gown, mask dangling beneath his chin.

"The operation is finished and, while we consider it a success, his condition is serious. He'll be moved to recovery shortly, then placed in ICU. But I think he's going to make it."

Those assembled gave subdued cheers. The surgeon flashed them a tired grin before bustling off.

"Once he gets in a private room, I'll need to see him." Alex spoke to Agent Matterling, who gave a guarded nod. "Here's my cell-phone number. Call me as soon as he's moved."

"He'll remain under heavy sedation."

"Good. He needs to be."

Matterling turned to go. Two men, both junior agents by the look of them, stepped up to flank each side.

A moment later, the other doctor touched Lyssa's arm, motioning her to step away from the others. Exchanging a worried look with Alex, Lyssa did as she asked, with Alex right at her back.

A moment later she had her answer. The woman doctor forced a smile. "This might not be what you want to hear, but you're definitely pregnant." Her certainty grated on Lyssa's nerves. "The best estimate is a late-September baby."

Baby. Lyssa wanted to give the woman a fake smile as she accepted her congratulations, but couldn't. The best she could do was accept her hug, and try to fix her attention anywhere but on Alex.

A baby. Alex's baby.

"I need to sit down." With shaky steps, Lyssa made her way to a chair and dropped into it. Still murmuring congratulations or instructions—Lyssa couldn't focus enough to tell which—the doctor clapped Alex on the shoulder and shook his hand before she left. Lyssa stared after her, avoiding looking at Alex, avoiding looking anywhere but at her own hands, clenched tightly together in her lap.

A moment later, Alex joined her.

"What do you want to do now?" he asked quietly.

She couldn't think. "I don't know."

They sat together in silence and while part of her blessed him for it, another part of her wanted to lash out at him. Despite his understanding, he hadn't told her what he was before marrying her, before making love with her.

Still, to be fair, he *had* used protection. Every single time, except in the shower.

When he slipped his arm around her shoulders, she held herself stiff. "All I ever wanted was a normal life."

He nodded. "House in the country, white-picket fence?"

The sound she made was not a laugh, exactly. It was way too bitter for that. "Yeah. Two kids, a minivan…" A husband who would stay. She had to cover her mouth with her hand to keep from saying the rest. Now was not the time to fall apart. She had decisions to make. She needed more information.

"Alex?" Swiveling out from under his arm, she sat on the edge of her chair and faced him. "Medication aside, what will this child—I believe you used the word *changeling*—be like?"

He didn't pretend to misunderstand. She gave him points for that. "Actually, we call them halflings. Most of them are born with the ability to shift."

Oh God. Her child, her little boy or girl—a wolf. Relentlessly, she forced herself to go on.

"Do your people fully accept them? Or are they outcasts, never quite fitting in either world?"

"My people—" he started, drawing his lips back in what looked more like a grimace than a smile. "The Pack welcomes them with love."

Sadness echoed in his voice, an emotion she didn't really understand at first, coming from him. Until he spoke again. "But will you?" Intensity blazed from his gaze. "How will you feel about this child, our child?"

He came closer and she saw matching shadows darkened his eyes.

How to answer? Still, she kept her hand cupped protectively over her abdomen. "How will I feel?" A surge of wonder filled her. She took a deep breath, willing herself to find calmness, normalcy, somewhere, somehow. So much had changed—and from this day on her life would be inexplicably tied to his world.

Despite all that, *she* hadn't changed. "This baby is mine. Boy or girl, human or—" she swallowed "—shifter, I will love him or her just the same."

He searched her face. Whatever he found there seemed to satisfy him, for he nodded.

Pregnant.

Since reaching adulthood, she'd imagined it—her own family, a loving husband, a red-cheeked baby. But in her wildest dreams, she'd never imagined any of this. She'd always thought it would be different than this, more joyful.

But then she'd never in a million years imagined she'd have been pursued by a serial killer who'd believed by killing her he could bring her to immortal life.

And she'd never imagined she'd be carrying the offspring of a werewolf.

Chapter 14

"I need some time alone." She looked away as she spoke. "To think."

"But—" Alex started to protest.

"The Bone Man's dead." Her voice came out sounding surprisingly weary. "I'm not in any danger."

Without waiting for him to agree, she started off down the hall. Taking the elevator to the first floor, she smiled at the disinterested receptionist and kept going.

Once outside, she stopped and breathed in the fresh late-April air. It smelled like rain. Above, the darkening clouds roiled. In the distance, lightning flashed. A few seconds later, thunder boomed.

A storm drew near. A good gully-washer from the looks of it.

How fitting. Every bit of her old life was gone, washed away. She had no home, no business, and no best friend. She needed to mourn Marilee, and try and figure out a way to honor her best friend's memory.

But right now, she couldn't think. She needed to simply feel, to soak in the unjust miracle of being alive while Marilee, kind-hearted, generous Marilee, was not.

Large drops of rain began to hit her arms and splatter the pavement. Lifting her face to the sky, she kept walking, welcoming the rain and letting it mingle with the tears that streamed down her face.

As she rounded the corner, the shower became a downpour. Drenched, she kept going. In the parking lot to the side of her, people rushed from their cars to the hospital entrance, most without umbrellas. Lyssa kept her pace measured, glad the roar of the storm drowned out her sobs.

At the rear of the hospital was a field, then the edge of forest. Though the back of her neck tingled a warning, she crossed the grass, unafraid of the lightning that danced around her. After all that had happened, she dared lightning to strike her.

At the edge of the trees, she glanced back at the hospital. The heavy rain blurred her view. She only saw the fist right before it smashed into her face. She didn't even have time to scream.

For the third time, Alex checked his watch. Lyssa had been gone a good half hour, and a late-spring thunderstorm raged outside. He wasn't really worried—after facing a horrible threat like the Bone Man, what possible danger could Lyssa face? He even understood why she'd wanted to be alone. In the space of a few hours, she'd not only found out she was pregnant, but she'd lost her best friend.

Lightning flashed again and he decided. Time to go find her.

He searched the second floor without success and then the first. The receptionist told him she'd seen Lyssa go outside.

"Did she come back in?"

The woman shrugged and went back to reading her magazine.

Outside. He went to the automatic doors, standing to the left of them so they'd stay closed. The storm appeared to be winding down. The rain was letting up and some of the gloominess seemed to be dissipating. Still... Surely Lyssa hadn't gone wandering around outside in *that*.

Standing just outside the hospital front door, he placed a call. The back of his neck fairly burned.

He took a step, then stumbled. Ran a shaky hand across his forehead, which was suddenly beaded with sweat.

"Lyssa." She was hurt—she needed him.

He ran.

Lyssa came awake to the sound of moans. Struggling to open her eyes, at first she saw nothing. Then, as her vision adjusted to the darkness, she could make out another form, trussed and tied next to her.

"Hello?" She tried a tentative greeting. "Are you all right?"

The moaning stopped.

"Lyssa?" A feminine voice, though weak.

Squinting into the dimness, Lyssa tried to make out the other woman's features. She looked like—no. She couldn't be. "Marilee?"

"Lyssa. Oh dear God, I pray it isn't you."

Marilee. She wasn't dead. A burst of joy shot through her. She tried to move, to embrace her friend, and couldn't. Confusion, then terror. Stark, horrible terror. Her hands were tied. Her hands, her legs—good lord, she was trussed up the same way as her friend.

"Who—?"

"He's crazy." Marilee's harsh whisper made Lyssa aware she'd spoken out loud. "You shouldn't have come." An odor—horrific, like rotting fruit or—she dared not think it—flesh—made her gag. "Where are we?"

"His den." Marilee sounded defeated. "Be glad it's dark in here. You don't want to see it when it's not."

Lyssa couldn't help but look around. Even in the dim light, she could see what looked like bones, gleaming. Bones, picked clean and bleached white, littered the ground.

She remembered what Alex had told her about copycats. Now that the Bone Man was dead, had some copycat grabbed Marilee and then herself?

"He's crazy," Marilee repeated.

"Who's crazy? Where—" she swallowed "—is he?"

"Who knows? He comes and goes." Marilee shuddered and drew a shaky breath. "Worse even than him, he has this pet wolf. It's vicious. Both of them are insane."

"Pet wolf?" Stunned, she couldn't think. "But the Bone Man's dead."

"We should be so lucky." Marilee sounded resigned, though horror still echoed in her voice. "He's not dead. Now he'll kill you as well as me. He wants our ribs—something about bringing us back to life for eternity. He's nuts. We'll die together now."

Not dead? "But the FBI—there was a shoot-out—they got him."

"Lies." Another voice, raspy and full of a wicked glee, came from the shadows. *Him*. She recognized the voice.

With an effort, Lyssa bit back her gasp. "How?"

"I found their van first. Before I killed the woman, I slaughtered them." He laughed, a horrifying sound that died off into a rattling cough.

"Then I took their phone, and hit Redial."

"You…" Stunned, Lyssa searched the shadows in vain. "You called Johnson. You told him you were dead."

"Yessssss," he hissed. "To bring you out into the open."

"Why me? Why Claire?"

"I thought Claire was my queen. But she didn't come back to life, even when I took her rib. But you—fierce and strong—married one of my own kind. I saw you together. You shouldn't have gone to him. You were looking for me. Me." He snarled the last word, the single syllable seeming to ricochet off the rocks surrounding them.

Horrified, Lyssa winced. "You've got it wrong. I'm not the one."

"We shall see, won't we?" His laugh was as awful as his snarl, making her shudder.

Her gun. What had happened to the weapon Alex had given her? She'd dropped it into her purse. A quick search revealed her purse was gone. She could only pray if the Bone Man had it, he hadn't found the gun. If she could get her hands untied, then locate her purse, she'd stand a chance of defending herself.

She might as well wish for a miracle. He wasn't going to let her live long enough to untie herself.

The only number he had was Trask's cell and no one answered. Cursing himself for not scribbling down Johnson's direct line, Alex climbed in his car and roared off toward the FBI building.

As soon as they buzzed him inside he had his answer.

The place was in chaos. Johnson looked like he'd been punched in the gut.

"The agents manning the van were murdered."

Alex closed his eyes. When he opened them again, Johnson was opening a roll of Tums. Popping two into his mouth, he offered them to Alex.

"No, thanks." Alex waved his hand away. "I came back because I can't find Lyssa. She's missing."

Johnson cursed. "The Bone Man isn't dead. In fact, it's highly probable he called me earlier, impersonating one of my men. One of my dead men."

Pulse kicking into overdrive, Alex clenched his hands into fists. He wanted to punch something, anything, and knew if Johnson kept talking, he'd probably take a swing at the younger man's face.

"You just confirmed my worst fear," he snarled, backing toward the doorway. "After killing several heavily armed FBI agents and the decoy, the Bone Man is still at large. And now, not only does he have Marilee, he has Lyssa as well."

"We're on it." Johnson stood, the bleak look on his face further validating Alex's words. "As we speak, a massive manhunt is being organized. The largest Ulster County has ever seen. We'll get this guy. Quickly."

"That's what you thought before." In the hall outside

Johnson's office, Alex stopped, judging himself far enough away that the agent was in no danger.

"We thought we had him."

"Yeah. And you were perfectly willing to accept Marilee's death, as well as the loss of your decoy and several men." Alex knew he sounded hard, out of control, but he was. "Tell me where the crime scene is. I know it's near Woodstock, but where?" He wanted to make sure it was the same location the Bone Man had left on Lyssa's voice mail.

Johnson hesitated. "I—"

"My wife is missing. Don't make me have to throttle the information out of you."

Straightening, Johnson rested his hand on the butt of his gun. "Are you threatening a federal agent?"

Alex looked from the gun to the man's face, letting a cold smile show on his own. "Johnson, *I* am a federal agent. But to answer your question, yes. I am." He took a step forward.

Swallowing, Johnson backed down. He rattled off directions. Some place. Except Johnson provided one piece of information that Alex hadn't known. "It's in a neighborhood."

"Near a residential area?" Alex cursed. "I can't see why he'd risk it."

"Maybe he lives near there. The showdown took place at an old abandoned rock quarry way back in the woods. It's got houses nearby, but it's pretty remote."

"Thanks." Alex growled out the word.

Removing his hand from his holster, Johnson inclined his head in a nod. "We're organizing a manhunt," he reminded Alex. "We can take care of it."

"Screw you and your manhunt." Alex turned to go.

"What are you going to do?" Johnson shouted after him.

Nearly to the exit, Alex spun. "What the hell do you think I'm going to do? I'm going after him. I'm gonna find the sick bastard, take him out, and rescue Lyssa and Marilee. It ends now."

"How?"

Ignoring Johnson's question, Alex pushed at the front door. The automatic lock held. Fury mounting, he directed a stare at the Plexiglas-shielded room, knowing deadly intent would show in his eyes and not caring. Play-nice-time with the feds was over. "Unlock this door now, or I'll bust through it."

In less than three seconds the buzzer sounded, letting him escape.

Outside, Alex slid into his car and roared off, fury heating his blood. Energy sizzled along his nerve endings. Soon, he would change.

Disregarding the posted speed limit, he picked up 9W and headed northwest. His wolf self roared under his skin, fighting for release, knowing the situation demanded it. It would be more difficult to change near a residential area, but it could be done. Correction, *would* be done.

The Bone Man had a big surprise coming.

After a series of increasingly convoluted turns, he located the neighborhood. The area where Johnson had said the quarry was located wasn't accessible by car, which was good. He pulled off onto the shoulder. He had a choice—gun and silver bullets with his human self, or razor-sharp teeth and brute strength as his wolf self.

Right now, he'd go in as a human. He could change later if he had to in order to save Lyssa.

Moving quietly, he set out into the trees. Dense undergrowth hampered the way. Twigs crackled underfoot, branches scraped and snapped. If the Bone Man had changed into his wolf form, superior hearing would alert him to Alex's presence long before he got there. But remaining a wolf so long used up a lot of energy. Alex was betting the Bone Man slept, building up strength for the next round.

Pressing on, ten minutes later he emerged from the forest to find a large, gray pit. He'd located the quarry.

"Are you going to kill us now?" Marilee's voice trembled.

"Marilee!" If her hands hadn't been tied, Lyssa would have thwacked her friend on the shoulder. "Don't give him ideas."

"It's what he's been saying since he grabbed me." Marilee sounded on the verge of hysteria. "As soon as he got you, he planned to do a dual rib-taking ceremony."

"Wonderful. That's just freakin' wonderful."

"And it will be." The Bone Man's voice seemed to echo off the rocks surrounding them, though Lyssa thought it was probably her imagination.

Fine. Lyssa stuck out her chin. No way was she going down without a fight. "Then let's get to it, shall we?"

"Lyssa!" Now it was Marilee's turn to admonish. "Have you lost your mind?"

The Bone Man's raspy chuckle prevented Lyssa from answering. "Amusing, both of you. And you who are my queen, I welcome your eagerness."

The hair on Lyssa's arms rose. He meant her. He thought her eager. Blech.

"But the ceremony shall be tonight, when the moon is full. I have need of her power." He yawned, and Lyssa could picture him stretching. Though she peered hard through the cave's dim light, he remained in the shadows and she couldn't make out his form.

She screwed up her courage. "Show yourself." She swallowed, remembering the name from Claire's tombstone. "I would see the body King Nebeshed has chosen."

He gave that awful laugh again, then made a tsk-tsking sound. "Patience, little one. We will stand eye to eye later, when my power has been restored and the time is right."

He meant when he took her rib. Lyssa closed her eyes, fighting nausea at the thought.

"I must rest." The Bone Man chuckled louder, almost a cackle this time. "Big night ahead."

Though she heard no sound to betray his leaving, after a few minutes of silence Lyssa realized the Bone Man had gone.

No way was she letting that maniac lay a hand on her. She had more than herself to protect. Alex's baby—the child of the man she loved.

Alex. Where was he? Never more had she wished the supernatural connection he'd believed in was real. Because she had no other options, she concentrated on that one small, slim hope. Though bringing him to her with a thought was no doubt as futile as connecting with Claire's dead spirit. Right now, that was all she had.

"I can't believe we only have a matter of hours." Marilee's whisper broke into Lyssa's thoughts.

"Until he comes back?"

"Yes. Do you have any idea what time it is, how long

we have until the sun sets? You heard him." Marilee sounded resigned. "Once it's dark and the moon rises, he'll be back. I wonder who he'll kill first."

"Why are you whispering?"

"I don't want him to hear us."

"Why does it matter?"

Marilee started to cry. "You're right, of course. He's going to kill us anyway, no matter what we do. As long as there's no torture involved, I think I'd like to go first. I don't want to have to listen to your screams."

Her fatalistic words made Lyssa struggle against her bonds. Her efforts were in vain. The tightly tied rope wouldn't give an inch. "Marilee, stop."

Ignoring her, Marilee sniffled. "Do you think it will hurt, dying?"

"Cut that out." Furious, Lyssa wanted to shout. Instead, she kept her voice measured, even. She refused to whisper. "I'm trying to figure out a way to get us out of here."

"How? We're both tied up. I haven't eaten for days. You don't—"

Tinny notes sounded from a few feet away. "Flashdance." Her cell phone. And her purse. With the gun still in it, unless the Bone Man had found it. Somewhere in the shadowy cave.

"What the...?"

"My phone. Alex is calling." Struggling against her bonds again, Lyssa tried to wiggle in the direction of the noise. "I need to get to it."

Trussed up so tightly her feet were numb, she only made it a few feet when the ringing stopped.

"Gone to voice mail," she said dully. "Damn it."

But a few seconds later, her ring tone began to sound again.

She startled to wiggle. Behind her, she could hear Marilee's harsh breathing. Her friend had stopped crying and now appeared to be focused on Lyssa and her cell phone.

Focus. Alex's word. Mentally, she tried to send out a message to him. She kept on wiggling, wincing as the sharp rocks cut her skin. Each inch, each half inch, she considered a personal victory.

On the sixth ring, the phone again went silent. A moment later, instead of the tinny tune of "Flashdance," her phone played "Hotel California." Claire's song. Her cell phone hadn't been set to play that song as a ring tone.

Impossible.

"How'd you do that?" Marilee asked. "How'd you make it change the ring tone?"

"I didn't." Hardly able to speak past the lump in her throat, Lyssa peered into the dark cave. Was this the promised signal? "Claire?" she whispered, "where are you?"

Six bars of the song, then silence. After a moment, the old Eagles song again filled the cave. This process repeated itself over and over. Ring tone times six, then stop. A pause. Then again.

"Claire's dead." Marilee sounded afraid. Lyssa realized her friend thought she'd lost her mind.

"I know." Lyssa couldn't help but smile. Her baby sister had let her know that she still existed, somewhere.

The phone chimed again. Welcome to the Hotel California.

"What's he doing?" Marilee asked, abandoning her whispering. "Why does he keep calling?"

"Alex is using the phone to lead him to us." Her heart raced. Again she struggled against her bonds. They held.

So she kept up her shimmying movements, ignoring the sharp stones, focusing only on the cell phone ringing in the darkness.

"What are you doing?" Sounding a little farther away, Marilee's voice came stronger, full of hope.

"Trying to get to my purse and the phone."

"Why? What's the point?" Marilee sounded petulant, like a small child. "Your hands are tied behind your back. Even if you can maneuver right on top of your purse, you can't open it, never mind getting the phone out."

Good point. Even if she could drag the purse close with her teeth, Lyssa couldn't get to the phone. Or the gun.

The last ring stopped. This time the phone fell silent.

What now? Lyssa closed her eyes for a second. Had Alex given up on her?

A rock skittered across the ground behind her. She turned her head, squinting to try and see what had caused the sound. A moment later, she had her answer.

A huge wolf walked into the cave, his silver coat appearing to glow in the murky light. The animal padded over near them, stopping a few feet away and sniffing the air.

"That's his pet!" Marilee gasped. "That beast is how he rips apart his victims and takes their rib. He's lied again—he's not waiting until sundown. He means to kills us now!"

Chapter 15

More lies. Heart pounding, Lyssa grimaced. She shouldn't be surprised. The last few years of her life had been colored by lies, first with Claire, then with her false marriage to Alex. It would be ironically fitting that she now die with a lie from her killer.

But not without a fight. No way would she roll over and become his willing sacrifice.

Frantically, she began pushing her body across the floor, toward her purse. Though what she'd do when she reached it she had no idea, reaching the purse became her salvation, her holy grail. Her focus.

Another sound. Closer. She pushed her scraped and battered body as hard as she could.

"Oh God, Lyssa—it's coming for you." Marilee began to shriek.

For the space of a heartbeat, Lyssa froze. She made the mistake of looking over her shoulder.

The wolf came closer. She got a better look at him, though shadows hid his head. The beast was huge. Maybe because of his size, the animal didn't slink or creep. He didn't rush, though he didn't take his time either. He simply padded, continually scanning the cave as though looking for something or someone else.

Another couple of seconds and he'd be on her. Breathing hard, she resumed her struggles. Despite her best efforts, she only gained a few feet.

She could feel the wolf's hot breath on the back of her neck. She pushed herself harder, arching her body up at the same time and trying to use her bound hands to push the animal away.

Another wiggle. Her chin brushed a soft lump—her purse! Now what?

Above her, the wolf growled. Slashed at her hands with his teeth. Rather than tearing her skin, the razor-sharp fangs cut into the rope that bound her.

Hope flared within her. She stopped struggling. No matter how slim the chance, she prayed for the wolf to free her accidentally.

The wolf slashed at her again. Still tied, her bonds loosened.

Abruptly, Marilee's cries cut off, mid-shriek.

Lyssa glanced back at her friend.

Another wolf, identical to the first, stood between her and Marilee.

Two wolves. That meant…one of them had to be Alex. He'd followed the sound of the cell phone. Lyssa looked up at the wolf that stood over her. Now she understood. Instead of attacking her, he'd deliberately tried to slash her bonds. He was trying to free her.

She arched her back, lifting her hands. "Hurry."

Alex's teeth slashed once more, tearing through the rope. She could move her hands.

The other wolf leaped forward, teeth bared.

Launching himself to meet the Bone Man's leap, Alex pushed at her with his hind feet. Instantly understanding, she rolled out of the way, hands free, fumbling for her purse.

The two wolves crashed together, snarling.

Lyssa groped inside her purse. Her fingers connected with the cloth-wrapped pistol. Pulling it out, she fumbled with the hammer, glad now Alex had insisted she carry it loaded. Edging herself until her back was against the stone wall, she hastily untied her legs and climbed unsteadily to her feet.

Roaring, the wolves rolled on the ground, fangs flashing. Blood spotted silver fur as they slashed and clawed each other.

Indistinguishable. She couldn't tell them apart.

Still tied, Marilee made a bleating sound, like a ewe watching someone slaughter her lamb.

Keeping one eye on Alex and the Bone Man, Lyssa moved over to her friend and crouched next to her.

"Marilee, pay attention. Listen to me now."

The awful bleating stopped. Unable to tear her eyes away from the horrible lupine battle, Lyssa switched the gun to her left hand, keeping it ready to shoot. Using her right hand, she fumbled with the tight knot holding Marilee's rope secure.

"Once your hands are free, I want you to untie your feet. Then run, run as fast as you can, away from here."

"What about you?"

Lyssa jerked her chin toward the gun. "I'm armed. Alex taught me to shoot. I'll be fine."

One final tug and Marilee's hands came free.

Pushing herself to her feet, Lyssa backed away. The wolves had moved apart. Each circled the other, darting in to slash with razor-sharp teeth, then out. Blood matted each wolf's fur. Their paws slipped in puddles of it on the stone floor.

Marilee freed her feet and stood, swaying. She looked at Lyssa.

"Go."

Needing no second urging, Marilee took off.

Neither wolf paid heed to the sound of Marilee's footsteps as she ran away.

There was so much blood, it was impossible to tell who was winning. Lyssa gripped the revolver with both hands, steadying it. She had to shoot one of them. But which one? God help her if she killed the wrong one.

The animal nearest her turned its head and bared its teeth, snarling. Blood dripped from his snout. The other wolf lunged forward, going for the throat. Connecting, he clamped his teeth and bit hard, holding on with savage force.

The second wolf yowled, shaking himself from side to side, trying to fight him off.

The first wolf held, ripping open the throat of the other. Blood spurted, more blood, covering each animal's fur so that silver looked crimson.

Lyssa's heart pounded. She couldn't hold the gun steady. Which one? If the Bone Man had Alex by the throat, she needed to save him. If the opposite was true, she could help.

She moved closer, looking for a clue, something, anything to let her know which one was Alex.

More blood—spraying her. Wiping her eyes, Lyssa moved closer still, her weapon in her hand, ready.

The second beast struggled, growing weaker. While a bite to the jugular would kill a normal wolf, Alex had said only a silver bullet or fire would kill a shifter.

Her heart pounded. Which one? Which one?

Then the first wolf, still gripping the second's throat, looked at her.

Alex's beloved amber eyes gleamed in the wolf's blood-soaked face.

Alex.

Without hesitation, Lyssa pointed the pistol at the other wolf. She squeezed the trigger. Shot. More blood spread over the Bone Man's already crimson chest. Cocking the hammer, she shot, aiming for the heart per Alex's instructions. She clenched her teeth at the recoil then repeated the process. Sight. Aim. Fire. She felt a savage flash of triumph as each silver bullet found its target.

Finally, the gun clicked empty. Four shots, as she hadn't left a bullet in the chamber.

Feeling like it burned her hand, Lyssa dropped the gun. She heard the echoing clatter as metal hit rock and kicked it away with her foot. She eyed the Bone Man, now limp in Alex's powerful jaws. Dead. Surely she'd killed him.

Alex released him. The dead wolf, the Bone Man, slid to the ground. Alex stood over the body. He lifted his crimson muzzle and howled. Somehow, she understood. Alex symbolically claimed his kill. How she knew this, she put down to the mysterious connection Alex had always claimed between them, which she now knew to be fact.

She took a step forward. Toward him.

Face coated with blood, Wolf-Alex stared at Lyssa. Trembling, breathing hard, she took another step. His silver coat was cut and bleeding, but even as she watched, the blood flow slowed and she remembered he'd said shifters healed faster than normal.

Legs wobbly, she moved closer. Slowly, painfully, as though she'd aged a hundred years in the course of four shots.

Alex watched her come, unmoving. He held himself alert, his bearing proud, though he favored one leg.

Her feet slid in the pools of blood. She fell, pushed herself up, and kept going.

When she reached Alex, she dropped to her knees. Uncaring of the blood or her clothes, she stroked his crimson-spattered fur, probing delicately for signs of serious injuries and finding none. He allowed this patiently.

Finally, when she'd finished, she threw her arms around his neck and buried her face in his fur.

"I love you," she told him, not knowing or caring if as a wolf he'd comprehend the words, but certain he'd understand the gesture. After all, actions spoke louder than words. So she herself had told him, when he'd returned to her following the Bone Man's first attack.

When she finally released him, her clothes were stained. But for the first time in months, her soul felt cleansed.

With a soft *whuff,* Alex cocked his head and licked her face. She closed her eyes and let him clean her, the feel of his rough tongue oddly soothing. The last remnant of the awful quaking inside her finally stilled.

When he'd finished, cool air soothed her face. She

opened her eyes and saw him moving away. As he reached the mouth of the cave, he turned his head and looked at her, and she could have sworn he smiled before vanishing into the woods.

Once more, she looked at her fallen enemy. The Bone Man began to shimmer then, the wolf form, though dead, changed into the body of a man. Dispassionately, she studied him. Though bloodstained and bruised, he looked like an ordinary man—tall and wiry and balding. He could have been a favorite science teacher or an accountant. He did not look the least bit like a serial killer with delusions of grandeur. Nor did he, she thought wryly, look at all like a werewolf.

Four hours later, the FBI was still trying both to clean things up and figure out what had happened. Though a hysterical Marilee first told them, and Lyssa corroborated, they couldn't get their minds around the idea of a second wolf attacking the first. And, because they had no wolf body, just a lot of blood, as far as they were concerned the women had suffered a hysteria-induced delusion.

The Bone Man's "pet wolf" was considered still at large, and a search was organized. Lyssa knew they'd find nothing, but couldn't tell them. The FBI finally released her to the local police, who'd taken her to a nice motel in Wicket Hollow and promptly scheduled a press conference in time to make the nighttime news. The biggest story of the year would go national. The serial killer dubbed the Bone Man was dead. Film at eleven. She'd had just minutes to get ready to be escorted back to the police station.

When the press conference was over, Lyssa, wrapped

in a blanket and sipping on hot tea, had told her story five times. Twice to the FBI, once to the state police, again to the locals, and the final time for the barrage of cameras. She'd stuck as close to the truth as possible, remembering Alex's earlier words. Though she still hated to lie, she now recognized that telling the truth wasn't always possible. This was one of those times to keep one eye closed.

A crash from the reception area made everyone turn. The Wicket Hollow police station was usually closed this time of night. Everyone in town knew that. The reporters had finally gone, having gotten their story, and the police were preparing to escort her to her motel room for the night.

Lyssa Reinholt-Lupe shivered. Not from cold, but because the back of her neck tingled a familiar warning.

"Not again," Officer Kane groaned. "That front window is brand new."

Alex strolled in, brushing off the two cops trying to apprehend him.

Lyssa's heart skipped as she met his gaze. "You didn't—?"

"I didn't break it this time. The door crashed a little loudly when I had to, er, persuade them to let me in." He gave her a wolfish grin.

The watching cops looked at each other, then at Alex. He waved them away. Moving in unison, all the officers complied, exiting the room without comment and closing the door behind them.

Pulling up a chair, Alex turned it around and straddled it, scooting close enough so their knees touched. He looked her directly in the face, his expression unreadable, except for the seriousness of his stare.

She met his gaze, putting all her emotions into her eyes. Love, trust, hope—all of what she felt. "I'm glad you came."

"How can you look at me like that?" His voice sounded hoarse. "Can you ever look at me again without remembering the savagery and blood, without thinking back to the horror of this day?"

"You saved my life," she told him. "And our unborn child's life, as well as Marilee's. What greater gift could you give me than that?"

He looked down, as though humbled. "Ah, Lyssa. You don't understand. My leave of absence will soon be over and—"

"Shhh." She put a hand against his lips. "There are a few things I need to say first."

He kissed her hand and waited.

"I've always hated lies. You know that."

"I—"

"Shhh. But I've come to realize if I've hated lies, how much more must you? Your entire existence is based upon pretending to be something you're not. No wonder undercover work came so easily to you."

Alex watched her, his expression thoughtful.

She took a deep breath, reaching for the courage to say the last, to give him the gift that loving him made possible. "You don't have to stay." The words came out in a rush. "Not for me, or the baby. Of course you can visit whenever you like, but I know how much your job means to you and undercover agents can't really have a family—"

He kissed her, silencing her. Then, when she drew a deep breath to continue, kissed her again.

"Lyssa, if you would let me finish, what I've been trying to tell you is that I'm giving the DEA my resignation. I want more than my job now. I want a family, a home, a white-picket fence around it. I want to be there for my child, to watch him or her grow. I want to be a father. And, more importantly—" this time he pressed a light kiss on the tip of her nose "—I want to be your husband. I want to go to bed every night curled into you, and wake every morning to your face."

Flashing her a smile, he uncoiled himself from the chair and pushed it away. He dropped to his knees in front of her, took her left hand and tugged off the scratched gold band they'd found at a pawn shop that Hades Claws had frequented two years ago.

From his pocket he pulled a small, green velvet box. Opening it, he slid the new platinum ring on her finger. A square-cut diamond solitaire winked up at her. She gaped at it, then back at him.

"Lyssa Reinholt-Lupe, will you do me the honor of really becoming my wife?"

Speechless, she stared at him while her eyes filled with tears. Not wanting him to see, she dropped her head.

"Don't cry, sweetheart." Voice cracking with emotion, he brushed a stray stand of hair from her face. "A simple 'yes' will do just fine."

"Yes," she finally said raising her chin in time to see a single tear run down his face. Wiping it away with her finger, she cocked her head. "Is it true what I hear about wolves? That they mate for life?"

"They most certainly do," he said, solemn.

"That's good enough for me."

Now laughing, he kissed her again to seal the vow.

* * * * *

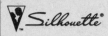

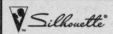

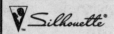

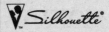

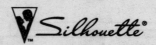

COMING NEXT MONTH

#1369 LOVING THE LONE WOLF—Ingrid Weaver
Payback

To keep his business, mulitmillionaire Nathan Rand needed to hunt down Russian gangster Stephan Volski. His plan hit a major snag when Nathan found himself falling for Kelly Jennings—Volski's girlfriend. Their mutual attraction was undeniable, but soon they'd have to decide whether their love was worth their lives....

#1370 MELTING POINT—Debra Cowan
The Hot Zone

When fire investigator Collier McClain and detective Kiley Russell were teamed up to uncover who murdered four firefighters, the attraction that ignited at a holiday party only grew deeper. But both were dead set on avoiding trouble, so no matter how hot their desire, their vows to keep things professional had no melting point—or did they?

#1371 DANGER CALLS—Caridad Pineiro
The Calling

Ever since Melissa Danvers became a vampire's personal physician, she'd had no time for a normal life, much less love. But when her experiments promised the key to eternal life, she knew her enemies would stop at nothing to steal her knowledge. Only the expertise of former lover Sebastian Reyes could keep her safe. Mixing business with pleasure was never smart—especially when danger was knocking on your door.

#1372 ONE MAJOR DISTRACTION—Linda Winstead Jones
Last Chance Heroes

When Flynn Benning and his team went undercover in an all-girls school to crack a robbery and murder case, he hardly expected to fall for school chef Tess Stanford. Although Flynn was keen on keeping his relationships casual, Tess was not a casual kind of woman. But once Flynn finished his mission, this one major distraction was sure to change his ways....

#1373 TRUTH OR CONSEQUENCES—Diana Duncan
Forever in a Day

SWAT guard Aidan O'Rourke was out to find the man who'd murdered his father. Not only did reporter Zoe Zagretti have what it took to solve the case, but Aidan felt a sizzling need for her. As the two came closer to avenging his father's death, deadly secrets were exposed...and so were their hearts.

#1374 DEADLY REUNION—Lauren Nichols
Bounty hunter Ike Walker was back in town to tell his ex-wife, Lindsay Hollis, that her brother might have been the victim of a cold-blooded murder. As the two worked to resolve the heart-wrenching crime, memories of their love took them down passionate paths they wanted to avoid—but what if the benefits outweighed the costs?